DAWSON CUMBERLAND

Thrill of Hope

First published by Dawson Cumberland 2025

Thrill of Hope is a work of fiction. All incidents, dialogue, letters, and all characters with the exception of some well-known historical figures are products of the author's imagination and not to be construed as real. Where real-life historical persons appear, the situations, incidents, and dialogues concerning those personas are entirely fictional and are not intended to depict actual events or to change the entirely fictional nature of the work. In all other respects, any resemblance to persons living or dead is entirely coincidental.

First edition

ISBN: 9798988141921

Cover art by Gracie Perry

This book was professionally typeset on Reedsy.
Find out more at reedsy.com

To the teachers that show us the music and the friends we make it with

For me, those were Matt Johnson, Josh Girndt, Jesse Russell, and Jonathan Lancaster

Conductor's Note

This piece is comprised of four distinct movements, with it's themes and motifs influenced by events in Boston, France, and other locales across history.

The first movement, *Allegro*, is to be performed in brisk, quick strokes. Primarily content exposition, this movement introduces our audience to the themes of the overall piece.

The second movement, *Adagio*, is to be performed with a slow elegance. Themes are explored with grace and control, outlining deeper meaning in the seemingly surface explanations from before.

The third movement, *Minuet*, is to be performed with moderate tempo, with steady grace. Variations of a ternary form occur as the piece slips almost into a dance of exploration.

The fourth and concluding movement, *Finale*, is to be performed lively, with an increased tempo and volume. A recapitulation of prior motifs designs an encompassing conclusion to the piece as a whole.

This piece is to be played with introspection and reverence, but above all else, mountainous hope.

Movement I: Allegro

Boston 2005

Decorations began to flood the halls of the symphony center the week following Thanksgiving. Charles finally felt the excitement wash over him as he descended the stark hallway of offices in the administrative wing to enter the first sections of ornamentation in the building. Christmas had always given him joy. Now that he was the lead administrator of the symphony, the past few years had been a Christmas dream come true. Not only did he get a front-row seat to witness some of the best musicians in the country rehearsing, but he also could casually walk through the Renaissance-style halls whenever he wanted. Now, with the season in full swing, he made it his duty to ensure that garland was strung, trees erected, and holiday spirit was on full display for the guests and staff alike.

Margaret had just finished hanging the new show cards when Charles spotted her. "Morn' Miss Margaret. Have a good Thanksgiving?"

She waved at him happily. "I sure did, got to spend it with my mother and aunt."

"That sounds relaxing, just the three of you."

Margaret raised a humored eyebrow. "You don't know my

mother and aunt."

Charles chuckled. He shifted his attention to the window card, remembering the proof he saw months earlier. It looked different in person, as they always did. He tilted his head slightly, studying the work as if for the first time. "You think it's too much?"

Both looked at the advertisement for a few moments, matching head tilts. The design was by no means minimal. But how could it be? There were nearly a dozen individual names to feature, along with other event information and holiday-inspired images. There wasn't a dull pixel to be found in the advertisement. But what else could one expect in an advertisement for a song's 150th anniversary concert?

Margaret opened her mouth to speak, but stopped herself short. "Too late to change anyway." She gave a wink, Charles amused by her candor.

He shrugged, nodding farewell. As he walked away, he called back over his shoulder brightly, "Go big or go home, as they say."

...

Bryn roughly massaged his temples. It was pointless, trying to rub the tension from his head through the sides. He knew since this was likely the fourth time he'd tried in the last hour. He was used to these tension headaches, normally bridging the gap from sleepless nights to uneasy stomachs, coming nearly each and every day. He had been staring at measure 48 for much too long, second guessing every note of his composition. *Why did he write a descending line for the strings here? And why didn't he have them working towards the third by beat four?* That was the obvious choice. Also, he worried the piece was building too quickly, giving the flow of the music no runway for the remainder of the song. But it was too late, since they were already months into rehearsals. He needed to focus on completing his notes for this afternoon's sessions.

The toll fogged his mind, making it difficult to focus and more unfortunately, difficult to relax. He'd found that through each onslaught of his own mind's making, the line between reality and tragedy continued to blur. Worse yet, the attacks had returned. None had taken hold in public, but it was only a matter of time. Just last week, something chipped away his defenses while he was conducting on the box. His hands tightened and his arms lost their fluidity. He only escaped by pretending to remember an appointment, ending rehearsal early to cover the spell. But that wouldn't work forever.

He was erasing a note that he had written when his phone rang. He rarely had calls in his office, so the sound startled him from focus. He quickly brushed eraser shavings from the score before sliding off the piano bench. He stood in front of his desk, lifting the phone from the receiver. "Hello?" he said.

"Bryn? It's Jordan Campbell, Mr. Marsh's manager. I believe we spoke once before."

"Ah yes, what can I do for you Mr. Campbell?" Bryn asked, stretching the receiver's cord as he returned to his notes.

"Well, there's no easy way to say this. James' mother passed away last night. She had been ill over Thanksgiving and took a turn for the worst. This isn't public news yet, but we wanted to let you know as quickly as we could."

Bryn stopped his scribbling. Sitting on the piano bench, he took in the gravity of the news. "I'm sorry to hear that. Please give James our prayers. I know how close he was with her. She had planned to be in attendance, which I know he was looking forward to."

"I'll be sure to pass that along, I know James would appreciate that. So obviously, he won't be able to rehearse adequately with the orchestra for some time. He thought it best to politely bow out of the performance so you could find a replacement soon."

Bryn inhaled sharply, not sure why the news surprised him as it did. "Oh, I see," he said in a constricted tone.

"He's disappointed to have to do it. He loved the challenge of working with the orchestra for the first time."

Bryn felt a small sense of pride in his orchestra despite the rising panic. "The feeling was mutual. Everyone here loved making music with him."

"I'll tell him that too, I know it would brighten his mood. He'll be canceling the rest of his regular tour to spend time with his fiancée and his brother back home in Oklahoma. Maybe keep him in mind for something down the road?"

Bryn nodded as he spoke into the phone. "Absolutely. Please send our condolences." He ended the call, nesting the handset in the receiver. As he did so, his eyes drifted towards the office window that shone brightly from the outside street lamps.

Before he let his worry fully overtake him, the worry of who or how to find a replacement or even how to tell Charles, he returned to the piano. Lifting the lid to expose the shining keys, his fingertips hovered above them. Then, in the solitude of his own office, he did what only seemed appropriate: with his music, he paid respect to those that passed and those left behind.

Roquemaure 1847

A new dusting of snow flurried from the carriage roof with each bounce of its uneven wheels. Placide Cappeau looked at the deserted street outside the coach, few windows still illuminated by any semblance of light. All he wanted, in the freezing lateness of the eve, was to be home in his own bed, but instead was going to church. Each time they passed a pile of cleared snow, he felt the chill of the night trickle down his spine. He should have declined Père Gilles as he frequently had, but for some reason his curiosity finally overpowered his disdain for the company.

Placide had been kept abreast of the information as he interacted with his neighbors and former church members in town. The church had undergone major renovations to its structure and amenities, he was told. Everyone said they were going to be absolutely divine when completed. "Heavenly", he was ironically told. As he made the usual pleasantries with others, each would always make an attempt to suggest he return to worship with them. Some were subtle, simply saying how much they missed seeing him at mass. Others resorted to more guilt-driven rhetoric.

By the time Placide's carriage reached the outside of the

church in Roquemaure, he'd made up his mind. He would stay long enough to see the renovations with his own eyes, keep the conversation intentionally light with Gilles, and promptly leave. The animosity that had festered between the two was sure to reignite if he stayed too long, so he planned to keep the visit brief.

As he stepped from the coach, mindful of the ice covered walkway, Placide noticed a large lump on the stoop beside the church doors. A closer examination revealed an unkempt man weighed by stacks of blankets and other fabrics, each tattered and in a terrible condition. When the man saw Placide walking slowly towards the church doors, he rose slightly to his knees, inching towards the new face. "Pardon me, Monsieur, but can you spare a franc?"

Placide took a step closer to the man, concerned by the request. "But, you're on the stoop of the Lord's house. Haven't you asked them? Surely they could give you a bed and even food."

The man spat on the wall behind him, the wall of the church. "They turned me away from their house, locked the doors to me. They have no help for us weary men."

Placide stared into the man's eyes, surprised by his answer. Without a word, he fetched a franc from his coat pocket and handed it over to the man, who took it without thanks. When Placide realized a thanks would not come, he walked to the church door and knocked.

"Monsieur Cappeau, I'm so glad you agreed to come. It has been too long," said Père Gilles. As Placide entered the church, shaking the snow from his collar, Père Gilles extended his right hand to shake Placide's. Both men silently stared at the hand, suspended between them, before Gilles' eyes flickered to the dangling cuff of Placide's right sleeve.

Placide waved off the concerned expression, nonchalantly. "Don't worry Mon Père, we'll just leave that to the Americans. No harm done." He patted Mon Père's arm as he walked through the foyer. "May I ask what this is about? I was surprised to receive your letter."

Père Gilles laughed. "Surely not as surprised as I was to hear your acceptance. A pleasant surprise, of course. Follow me into the sanctuary, I'd like you to see it as we talk."

Père Gilles opened the large, ornate doors that opened to the central aisle of the sanctuary. "A few things have changed since you last attended. We reupholstered the seating. We had the organ properly serviced finally. But of course, you probably have noticed the greatest alteration for yourself." He gestured his eyes toward the window that spanned the entirety of the rear wall of the sanctuary, behind the altar. In it, there was a glorious stained glass installation that reflected the interior lighting back onto itself in a dispersion of color.

Of course, Placide had already seen the glass. It was no less than four stories high, gallantly glistening in the evening candlelight. In fact, it had taken every ounce of him not to stare at the window the entire time he'd been in the sanctuary. It had been as grand as he'd feared and he hadn't a clue what to do when Père Gilles asked his thoughts.

The circular grouping of reds and deep purples around various portions resembled the petals of a rose weaving on vines. Each panel of glass was rich with the icon inclusions, holy and angelic, that he'd been expecting. The symbols that the church placed its weight on, overwhelmingly present. He feared that the longer his eyes scanned the piece, finding new touch-points to contemplate, his contempt would be in danger of becoming too obvious to Père Gilles.

Père Gilles took his silence as solemn adoration. "Beautiful, isn't it? The few that have seen it have all been moved by it as well."

Placide closed his eyes tightly, squeezing the moisture away along with the dread in himself that he found reprehensible. Was Père Gilles testing the waters this early? Had he so quickly forgotten one of the main tension points of Placide's dramatic departure? Placide turned his back to the glass to face Père Gilles directly. "Mon Père, I ask again: what is this about?"

Père Gilles could sense the attitude shift, slipping into a more careful tone. "We miss you here. I miss you here."

"I made my reasons clear. Obviously, there weren't any real changes," he said, gesturing to the stained glass.

Gilles glanced downward. "That's true. I've come to terms with our disagreements, for the time being. But I didn't invite you here tonight for us to rehash old arguments regarding penance or contributions. Certainly not to discuss worship order or creeds either. I asked you here because there are some opportunities arising. Your talents are greatly missed."

Placide's eyebrows raised with intrigue. "I assumed you already had a wine merchant," he said dryly.

Gilles gave a small, genuine laugh. "That we do. Your poems are what I was referring to. Your words. We still read some of the poems you left with us before. People continue to be moved by them." Gilles examined Placide's expression as he tried to avoid the priest's eyes. "You may have left our fellowship, but your imprints are still present." Placide's eyes tentatively found Gilles'. "I wanted to ask you to write one more. For Midnight Mass. This Christmas is a commemoration, and I think your words are the perfect thing for it."

Placide had begun to shake his head slightly, but Gilles continued his thought. "You could even work with Adolphe on it if you wanted. I'm sure he would enjoy that. Do you two still meet for drinks and poems at the cafe?"

Placide deflected the question, not raising his voice as his words slipped into those of challenge. "Tell me Mon Père, do you really trust me to write something appropriate for your services after everything we have said to one another in the past? Especially something you approve of for your special day?"

He waited for an answer which didn't quickly arrive. He waved his hand in defiance, fighting still to alter the subject from the request. "You know, I ran into the man you turned away outside. I find it difficult to write a celebration about the unified church when there's a man outside that you turned from these halls."

Gilles allowed the question to sit between them, breathing in its accusations fully before addressing Placide. He spoke gently, earnestly seeking peace. "We've welcomed Henri into these halls many times. He's been fed, clothed, given a place to sleep. But each time, he has stolen things from the church, even destroyed property. And we have always forgiven such actions. But during his most recent visit, he jeopardized Sister Catherine's safety, which I cannot allow. I asked him to leave."

Placide's cheeks flushed with embarrassment. His speed to accuse was usually his downfall, but this was one of the more disheartening examples. He sulked in the disappointment of himself for a few silent moments. "I'm sorry, I should not have said that. But I'm still not sure this is a good idea. Between our history, and of course my disdain for this whole remodel, I don't see a world in which I can do this. How could we ever even agree on content?" Placide began to walk towards the exit, turning over his shoulder to speak. "I pray you find what you're looking for."

"And I pray that for you, dear Placide."

Placide paused at the threshold because of the words, humbled yet again by the sincerity in their delivery. But the chill he felt fall down his spine from the outside air prompted him back to movement. He exited the sanctuary, swiftly boarding his carriage home. As the bounces of the coach's wheel rocked Placide's body, he found himself growing frustrated by the way the events had unraveled with Père Gilles. The audacity to request his poetry, to honor such a monstrosity of spending no less. As the coach began the final leg of its journey, he found a paper and pencil in the pocket of his overcoat. He began to aggressively scribble words, fueled by anger: *Midnight Christians...kneel.*

Boston 2005

T he conductor's box creaked and groaned under the weight of Bryn's constant shifting. He paid it no notice, impulsively checking his watch yet again. It was fifteen minutes after their scheduled rehearsal time and they still had not begun. He was known for his punctual rehearsals, rarely beginning late, especially this late. The musicians could feel his nerves, each curiously glancing to him, then to one another as they whispered among themselves during the holdup. He continued to hope that the replacement vocalist was stuck in traffic and requested the first chair lead an extra-long warm up.

As the final notes faded from the warm-ups, Bryn's nerves rose to his throat. They would have to begin rehearsal and catch-up the new vocalist whenever they finally arrived. His eyes drifted to the back auditorium doors once more, hoping to conjure their arrival. Instead, he saw Charles quietly slipping into the back row. Their eyes locked for a moment before Charles shook his head in a silent answer to the question on each of their minds.

Bryn stood straight, no longer leaning on the bar and clapped loudly to gain everyone's attention. "Alright, let's get started. No need to keep wasting your time. I've got some updated performance notes that I'd like to cover." He opened his folder, finding the first set of markings. "We're starting with the Scherzo piece, measure thirty. Horns, this one's for you."

He hesitated long enough for everyone to locate the charts in their own binder and raise their pencils. When he saw eyes, he continued, "I love your entrances there, keep punching it hard. But we're going to diminuendo much more dramatically, dropping to piano by beat three. And by the end of that measure, your volume should be near nonexistent. I only want strings at that point. So it should be one" he stomped for beat one, "two", clapping for beat two, "and off. Got it?" They each scribbled, murmuring their understanding.

As Bryn opened his mouth to address the strings, the rear auditorium doors crashed open as a group entered the hall. Many musicians jumped at the jolting sound, their concentration broken. A violinist dropped her bow, it bounced crudely across the stage.

All heads turned to the creators of the sound. After the initial shock, the whispers began as recognition settled on the musicians. By that time, Gregory Hall was already halfway down the aisle. His walk was slow and deliberate, completely aware of the impact his presence had; soaking every ounce of the coveted attention. Once he had walked the length of the auditorium, nearly reaching the stage, he gave a practiced, sheepish grin. "Sorry I'm late."

Nobody moved, their surprise still rendering them motionless. Instead, they stared at each movement, transfixed. It was a curious thing, the way everyone gawked at their first glance at a man that moved like them and spoke like them, but they had somehow determined to be separate from them.

Hall ascended the stairs, sauntering to center-stage to address the orchestra. He smiled, reveling in the recognition. "Hey everyone, Gregory Hall." It was then that he mistook the pencil being held by a violinist as a request for an autograph, which he happily snatched, signing the center of her score. Nobody corrected him, too stunned to speak.

Bryn descended the platform and greeted Hall, breaking the awkward tension. "Well, we're glad you're here. I'm Bryn, the conductor." He extended his hand.

Hall looked around quietly, then at his watch. "So should we start? Tight schedule of course."

Bryn retracted his outstretched hand awkwardly, continuing with great effort to appear hospitable to the new guest. "We were working through the show in song order, so if you want to take a seat and listen for a bit…"

Hall shook his head. "I can't stay for too long. You know how it goes, places to be and people to see." He looked to his team for support. "My guys tried reaching out to let you know I could only stay a short time, but they didn't get an answer."

"Funny enough, I had the same experience trying to contact you," said Charles, who had migrated to the action, unnoticed. He had seated himself in the front row, a serene expression on his face.

Hall laughed nervously as he understood the lie he'd been caught in, but still deflected. "Well, you know how it can be with these venues. Maybe the calls just never found their way."

The orchestra fidgeted uncomfortably as they understood the implications of what both Hall and Charles had said. But unsurprisingly, Charles remained calm and collected, waving a hand as if to brush off the whole thing. Bryn then took the opportunity to regain some type of control, remounting the platform. "Alright then, let's switch over to *O Holy Night*, starting at measure eight."

He addressed Hall quietly. "I'll cue you in on the downbeat of nine." Glancing at Hall's empty hands, he was concerned he hadn't received the music either. "Do you need a copy of the music?"

Hall shook his head, removing a small notebook from his pocket. "No need, got it all right here. Take it away."

Bryn raised his baton, speaking a soft count to himself as his hands assumed the tempo. *One, two, three, and...*

The orchestra began masterfully. When they reached the end of measure nine, Hall was happy to hear them execute the performance notes, making space for the vocalist's entrance. Bryn cued Hall, his pulse quickening in anticipation.

Hall began, "O precious night, the stars are brightly shining, it is the night of our rich holiday."

Brows began to furrow, confused by the altered lyrics. He was obviously reading something from the little notebook, Bryn could see as much from his short glances. But everyone wondered what obscure version he had come across.

"Long lay the world, from coast to coast sing loudly, as bells ring out and old St. Nick arrives."

Bryn swiped his hand across his body to stop the playing. Unlike most cutoffs which dwindle to an end, this one stopped instantly. The entire auditorium curious and horrified to know where such words had come from. The whispers and wild, questioning glances continued to increase as the tension too kept building.

Bryn waved Hall over in a small gesture. Turning his back to the musicians, he tried to speak quietly to keep the conversation private. Unfortunately, Hall's voice either could not or would not fall to a more confidential volume. "I think you might have gotten the wrong lyrics. Let me get you a spare…"

"Oh no, they're the right ones. I understand the confusion, but I went ahead and gave them a little update." He spoke proudly, as if he had anticipated the question and knew it only needed his simple explanation. When he wasn't immediately praised for his initiative, he kept speaking. "I just thought it needed some appeal for a wider audience, a holiday song for everyone."

Bryn hesitated to respond, noticing the frustrated murmurs of the musicians as they also overheard the answer. He scratched his face, buying time to find a diplomatic tone. "This is a classic, traditional song that has been respected and performed for over 150 years. It's the focus of this whole concert, the commemoration of its translation to English. It's loved and well-known. We can't just change the lyrics."

"That's my point though, it's old and outdated. Now it's modern, for everyone."

Bryn's eyelid fluttered in a subtle, unintended twitch as his cheeks flushed. "That's what *White Christmas* and *Jingle Bells* are for. But Christmas exists because of the Christian tradition. A tradition that countless people share, that is central to the very essence of their idea of living, people including myself."

Hall was oblivious to the aggression stirring in Bryn as he continued, less tactfully, "Listen, I'm just trying to liven it up. Make it a little more interesting than just a baby being born thousands of years ago in the Middle East."

Bryn inhaled, ready to open the floodgates when Charles stood quickly and addressed the room. "Hey, let's take five. Stretch your legs, use the restroom, do whatever." With hushed tones, he motioned to Bryn, "A word."

Bryn hesitated long enough to regain his composure. He left the platform to meet Charles at the side-stage steps.

"Listen, I agree with you, but this isn't the kind of discussion that should turn into a spectacle. I know you're under a lot of stress, but I think the best thing to do is finish this rehearsal peacefully. The musicians can't see volatility. You're the captain, give them poise and stability. You set the tone."

Bryn's expression exposed his defensiveness, but he tried to remain receptive. He knew Charles had a point. "I thought I kept cool," he said dryly.

Charles raised an eyebrow, smirking. "You really think so?" He nodded towards Bryn's hands, each held a half of his baton. Bryn examined the pieces, not having noticed the break until then.

"Must have slipped. Faulty wood or something," Bryn offered humorously.

Charles emphasized his point again, "Make it through this session. Let everyone get acquainted. Leave it to me to talk to Hall. You take the music. I'll play babysitter."

Bryn breathed deeply as his eyes drifted upward, searching for something in the ceiling ornamentation. "The lyrics are part of the music. They are the foundation for the whole thing. They're pure poetry. I mean, half my arrangement directly plays on what the words are saying or implying. I'm trying to convey the glorious sovereignty in those words." He knew when he met Charles' eyes that he too understood the importance, which comforted him.

"I know. That's why it's so important to handle this tactfully. Just let me talk with him."

Bryn pointed with one of the baton halves. "Then you might want to move fast. Looks like someone's leaving."

Charles turned quickly, jogging after the crew swiftly as he called to them. "Wait, where are you going? Hey, excuse me?"

One of the large men who had yet to speak paused, turned, and finally did so. "Mr. Hall has an interview downtown."

"But he just got here." Charles shifted his address to Hall. "You only sang for a minute."

"I told you, I can't stay long," Hall said, amused by Charles' sprinting after them.

The group continued through the door with Charles trailing behind them.

Feeling the residual frustration that began to plant its roots, Bryn gripped the handrail as he sat on the side-steps. His mind ran through each and every disaster scenario for the concert now that Hall had been introduced to the mix. He closed his eyes as each floated into focus, one after the other like a reel of slides shifting frame by frame.

"Come on buddy," Charles said, having returned and composed himself. Bryn nodded, his friend returning him to the rehearsal, if only for the time being.

Boston 1855

Opinions flowed passionately during the morning briefing for the Journal. That was the trouble with gathering this many music critics in one place; everyone had their opinion that was highly valued by their own audience. To add validity, their discernment in opinion and articulation of taste were reinforced by a paycheck each month. John hadn't been running the publication forever, but days like these made it feel that way.

"Williamson is just imitating all the standard motifs of the Renaissance. There is nothing new in what he's doing," Alexander said.

"Could you be more daft? Obviously he is appropriating those styles but shifting the focus of his pieces to farmers and other trades. A workers portrait, if you will. He's bridging old and new," Otto responded, raising the volume a touch.

"You only know that because it's what he writes in his composer notes. How is the average listener supposed to know any of that? It's not like he's using modern techniques to tie it all together. It's as much about the modern working class as my knit tie!"

It was after Alexander's pronouncement that the room

erupted in dissent. John had allowed everyone to speak for a few moments, gauging a sense of their differing opinions. After he had heard enough, feeling the shift from constructive to combative, he spoke firmly for each to hear. "Quiet men, quiet now." Everyone hushed, ears attuned to his voice. He exhaled loudly and slowly, as if willing everyone else to do the same decompression.

"None of us are strangers to the subjectivity of art. It is why many of us love it. That's why we all have work here; because if it wasn't subjective, you couldn't give your specific opinions on what it all means. What means something to me could be worthless to Alex. But what we cannot, will not do, is belittle someone's art merely because we do not understand it or hear what we were told to." He looked around the room, all eyes locked, hungry for his every word. "It's ok to not understand, and even say so. But we cannot afford to alienate artists by publishing something that could damage them permanently. We carry influence: we must carry it responsibly. Alex, write about what the piece meant to you. Simple as that. Mention not understanding it. But don't degrade it."

Alexander nodded his understanding, though his face indicated he was mildly disappointed by the decision. John waited another few moments, allowing space for any questions. Seeing that there were none, he checked the clock. "It would appear we are now twenty minutes over our scheduled time. If nobody has anything to add, shall we adjourn?" He noticed everyone gathering their papers silently. "Perfect. Thank you gentlemen."

One by one, the men filed out of the small, drafty conference space. Each made a special point to shake John's hand as they bid farewell. Once the room had fully cleared, John adjusted his spectacles and glanced at Alexander's draft once more. He'd heard the piece too; the music was dull and heavy handed. But he knew anything beyond a simple assessment should be formed by the listener.

Folding the pages, he slid them into his bursting folio barely able to close. Inside were dozens of other drafts, scrap papers, notes, music sheets, and his personal writings. Frankly, the only thing keeping any of it in place was the firm hand John kept clenched around the spine. Even that presence could fail eventually.

He shuffled down the hallway with his bundle, nudging the door of his office open slowly with his hip. He entered, walking to his desk as he felt the folio begin to slip from his grasp. He barely managed to get to the desk corner before his grip failed, sending the bundle slamming into a stack of mail, toppling the combined contents to the floor. He sighed, crouching to pick up the papers. As he knelt, one envelope caught his eye; a large brown one with a long carriage track crackled across the front. Leaving the other pages on the floor, he stood, examining the envelope.

It was addressed to him personally, with no return address. However, the postmarking signaled that it originated from France. John took his letter opener from the desk and opened the envelope in one swift, fluid motion. Inside, there were a few pages of sheet music along with a letter. Atop the page, a title read: "Cantique de Noël".

He flipped back to the letter, written in French. He knew French well enough, having performed many translations of various pieces in his time. It read:

"Dear John Sullivan Dwight,

I pray this message finds you in good health. I am an admirer of your Journal, and have been for some time. I wanted to pass along some music you may not be familiar with. This piece has touched many lives here in my country, but officials in the church have deemed it improper for worship and removed it. I hope you see its merit better than they. I too pray it finds continued life and enjoyment abroad in America and beyond.

Let it play on!"

John reread the note, as if hoping to further discover the identity of the anonymous author through their message. He shuffled to the first page of the score, seeing it written in French. His excitement waned slightly. Music had always been a bit more difficult to translate. Not only did the message have to come across, but so did the rhythm and tempo, syllables hitting in the appropriate measures. He rounded his desk, taking a seat. Tearing a page from his notebook and adjusting his spectacles, he began jotting down the short phrases.

Holy Night...savior's birth...soul...worth...

Before he could find his focus, a knock at the door interrupted him. "Come in," he spoke loudly. His secretary poked her head in, lightening his mood. "Oh, hello Harriet."

Harriet nodded passively. "Sorry to interrupt, but you're late for your lunch appointment with Mr. Rooney."

John jumped from his desk. "Oh yes, I'd completely forgotten!" He raced past Harriet, leaving the note on his desk and the rest of the papers strewn across the floor.

...

Hours later, John returned to his office. The lunch had taken longer than expected, causing him to run from meeting to meeting long into the late afternoon. Most days, he would be exhausted by the fast pace of his schedule. Today, he found himself invigorated as he once again sat at his desk to examine the music. He had spent most of his afternoon thinking about the possibilities in his head. Hungry to return to the challenge, he raised his pen.

Holy night, the night of our savior's birth. The world lay, in sin and mistake...

John furrowed his brow, cut by the realities held in just those short lines. This seemed to hint at the sentiment that Christ was born on Christmas, and that was a holy and sacred night. It also acknowledged the world in a simultaneous state of mistake and fault. The comparison was powerful, and he only had the first two lines.

He came and the soul felt its worth.

Christ showing a blackened soul the full potential, the essence of what one can be with redemption. Not worth founded in oneself, from Church ordination, or even from paid penance, but by granted grace.

Fall to your knees

John ran a hand across his tightly cropped hair, feeling sweat dampening it. His mind sparked from excitement for the new piece. But why had such a piece been sent to him specifically? He selfishly imagined how life could have been if such a piece had arrived earlier in his life, especially during his short time in ministry. He envied the economy in which the writer had composed such power from so few words. Christ's heavenly answer to mankind's most egregious follies. He had never conveyed such insight, he was sure of it.

His eyes quickly hovered over the third verse as he readied himself to translate, but he paused as he saw a word he had not expected: 'slave'. He felt light pinpricks touching the back of his neck, mild concern paired with the curiosity that the presence of such a word had kindled within him. Of course, the word had grown heavily charged the past few decades, especially in America. What could the French have used it as? He continued, eager to find out.

Truly, He taught us to love one another, His law is love, His gospel peace

Love and peace, a shared invocation for all who live, manifested through His law and His gospel. The perfect unity represented by unifying both the old and new teachings set in the Holy Scriptures.

He breaks chains, the slave is our brother. All oppression ceases in His name

John hovered his pen, mind racing further. He sat back slowly in the desk chair, taking a cautious breath. He loved the way the boldness came by surprise. To have the sentiments he had been advertising so repeatedly through the years put to music for worship made his heart swell. But despite the visceral emotion it caused, he questioned if he should publish the finished project. He had considered the possibility when he opened the letter, and had nearly decided to do so by the end of the first verse, but now he wavered. He feared what such boldness would do to the Journal's reputation; its security. He had a responsibility to the Journal's well-being without jeopardizing its quality. But he also felt a responsibility to make this song heard, without altering the message.

He had learned on many occasions that placing his own beliefs openly within the pages of the Journal could hurt the readership, decreasing sales that placed a strain on the staff. The last time he mentioned his abolitionist opinions was nearly two years ago, and it took the Journal months to recover their readership. This song was even more pointed than his messages had been, and he feared what the repercussions could mean for the staff. The Catholic church was a large presence of their readership, and he guessed they would likely take the first offense.

But his heart continued to pull him towards wonder; towards duty. How many people needed to hear this? He imagined how it would feel for such lines to be read by one who faced such oppression and persecution. Imagine a major publication lifting up a song the French church decided to forbid that spoke of loosened chains and Christ's redemption, bridging us all as brothers and sisters. His head ached as his inner voices conflicted with one another, beating and bludgeoning his skull.

What harm could come from simply translating the piece, even if only for himself? He needn't rush to publish or even forget the beautiful piece. This thought quieted his concerns for a moment. John retrieved his French/English dictionary from his bookshelf and found a new sheet of paper. He would translate the lyrics and proceed from there. As he breathed deeply, silently praying for the Divine hand to guide him, he carefully wrote atop the page: *O Holy Night.*

Roquemaure 1847

Placide Cappeau paced with such repetition and vigor, he could have worn a sunken path between his study and living room. He should be doing his actual job, the job that pays for his everyday life. But he couldn't shake the lines that he had scribbled during his carriage ride the night before.

Midnight Christians, it is the solemn hour,
When God as man descended unto us
To erase the stain of Original Sin

Placide had since completed the verse unable to sleep the entire following night.

And to end the wrath of his Father.
The entire world thrills with hope
on this night, that gives it a savior.

Not yet writing the conclusion, he already had the scrambled refrain bouncing around his head. He hesitated, struggling with himself as he considered if he could or should continue. He was almost certain that if he continued, he wouldn't be able to stop until it was completed. What then?

If he stopped now, he could toss the scraps in the fireplace, the memory floating away in the ash. Only he would know of the poem's existence. It could easily end as the whole thing had begun: within the confines of his consciousness. But he had been writing long enough to know that the words wouldn't leave him easily.

If he were to continue, to search for the rest of this idea a little longer, how would it end? The obvious answer would be to hand it over to Père Gilles, fulfilling the request that had borne the poem. But he had an inkling that the lyrics wouldn't hold the sentiments either man expected. The words wouldn't be what Monsieur l'abbé requested; even further from what he wanted.

Fed up with his own indecision, Placide snatched his glove and coat from the chair they rested on. He exited his home, no destination in mind, appreciating the vacant walkways that were blanketed in fresh snow. The sharp gusts of air blurred his vision with tears as he tucked his chin into his scarf. Walking had always helped his mind focus. He found that if he managed to lose his way, he usually found his mental path soon after.

As he walked, he turned over the possibilities of publishing in his head. He still found himself concerned with what Père Gilles might think, even after having left the congregation. But if he stepped lightly from the fear of hurting Mon Père, he might betray himself. The lines that ran through his head felt fluid and freely written, as by a Divine pen. He had never composed a piece so rapidly. The assurance that delivered the words was intoxicating. When he let himself breathe, appraising the small voice that spoke this creative symphony in motion, he recognized the work of the Lord in the composition.

After walking for much of the afternoon, Placide returned to his home to finish the piece by lamplight. The haze of quietly falling ice outside his study window lulled him into a deep focus.

He finished by nightfall, signing the bottom of the page for good measure. But fear for the power of his own words made him fear the pages, causing him to twice fold them and slip them into an unmarked envelope. Something about placing the pages out of sight felt safer.

But why fear power if it has it's strength in virtue? He had written words of praise, of hope, describing deliverance from the inherent perils of man. Words of conviction, pleas of humility and surrender, warnings of pride. He even found himself writing of equality, servants of brotherhood, and the credit for redemption. As he stared at the blank envelope, he tried to find the perfect title to represent the totality of its contents. He lifted his pen, certain in the simplicity of his labeling as he wrote the words *Midnight, Christians.*

...

Moving quickly to complete the piece, Placide paused when challenged with the next steps. The usual fear of having others read his work was doubled by the fear of the implications of Père Gilles or other church members reading it. He kept the pages close, quite literally, carrying the envelope in his breast pocket. But keeping it physically close served to keep its existence close to his thoughts.

"Have you been working on any pieces?" asked Adolphe Adam, Placide's close friend who still attended the church. The two were close, despite Placide's public separation from the congregation. Adolphe had always been understanding without vocally judging or pressuring Placide. But Placide's face had been showing the signs of his wandering mind, which is why Adolphe changed the subject of their jobs to something he thought Placide would find more enjoyable.

Placide shifted in his chair nervously. "Why do you ask?"

Adolphe cocked his head in inquisition. He had struck a nerve, though unintentionally. He liked getting his friend stirred up like this. "Oh, I've come to realize that you're always working on something. You're just too reserved to ever bring it up until I pry it from you. It's so tiresome," he said, rolling his eyes in jest.

Placide took the bait. "I'm not always working on something. You know, I have a career that takes most of my time. I don't often have the chance to scribble little notes despite what you might think."

Adolphe nodded, a faint layer of instigation entering his tone. "Ah, of course. And I'm sure Père Gilles hasn't asked anything of you either, anything that would prompt some pen-work of retaliation."

Placide's jaw dropped, utterly surprised by the quickness in which Père Gilles had spread word of their meeting. "So the old collar didn't hold his tongue?"

Adolphe gave a short laugh before sipping his drink, intentionally taking his time to answer the question. "Dear, prideful Placide, always worried about perception. Père Gilles asked me to write a piece, but I suggested he reach out to you instead. He didn't say so, but I could tell by his reaction that you'd already declined. He didn't say a thing." He noticed Placide's continued gaze, begging to know the whole exchange between Adolphe and Gilles. Adolphe obliged. "I told him you were an exceptionally better word-crafter than I, and that I would only work in tandem with you, not without."

Both men sipped their drinks in attempts to pass through the silence. Adolphe was thinking of the new windows at the church. Placide was confronting the frustration and gratitude that his dear friend had sparked within him. Against his better judgment, Placide slowly retrieved the envelope from his jacket, sliding it across the table to Adolphe. Adolphe's eyes ignited with excitement.

"So it did find you then…"

Placide blinked quickly. "Found me?"

Adolphe examined the pages he'd removed from the envelope. "Divine inspiration. Holy Spirit. Artistic disruption. Take your pick. But it pops up in moments like these. It hit me." He removed a scribbled sheet from his own pocket, holding it up to show his friend the messy music notations he'd made. "Woke up in the middle of the night with this arpeggio repeating in my head. Finished the bones of a score this morning."

It was Placide's turn to laugh. "So what was all that noble talk about not doing this without me?"

"Like I said, you're always writing. You just make me pry it from you."

Placide nodded his understanding. He remained silent, allowing Adolphe to read the lyrics deeply. He continued to dwell on the situation, the uncommon genesis of their respective works. "Funny how those they persecuted within their ranks are the ones burdened with making this for them. Leaves a bad taste, doesn't it?"

Not looking from the pages, Adolphe's brow furrowed. "That's a bit dramatic. They're not trying to burden us, nor do I feel burdened. This is what I love to do, and I know you love it too, despite what you want to admit. I actually think this is a sweet vehicle for some reconciliation between you and Mon Père. An olive branch of sorts."

"Some olive branch. Especially after our history. You are quick to forgive. I don't know how you can forget the terrible, prejudiced rumor they concocted about you. Even nonmembers joined in on it."

Adolphe looked to his friend sympathetically, not wanting to feed his anger further. "Nobody knows where that rumor started, and Père Gilles even spoke out against it. You don't have to use him as your scapegoat." Adolphe removed his spectacles, folding them and placing them on the table. He took a deep breath, centering himself. "Placide, sometimes I think you forget that we are all imperfect, and that our imperfections can cause others pain. But we commune not to achieve perfection, but to strive towards it together, even through the setbacks and tumbles. Don't take the slights against you as attacks. It's just human failure. Like you, they also have not achieved perfection.

"The only perfection there is is the Rule of God, which I know you still believe in. Just look at these verses." Adolphe held the page up. "Try to help others see it too, but don't expect people to reflect it perfectly."

They sat for some time, Placide's eyes fixed to the table, Adolphe staring at Placide. It was Adolphe who once again spoke, a lighter, more cordial air in his voice. "I must leave, but I'm glad we spoke. This poem is astounding. Do you mind if I hold onto it for a day or two?"

Placide shook his head without speaking.

"Very well. I'll see you soon. Take care, old friend."

Texas 1864

T he woods were damp, easy to navigate in the full-moon glow of the late evening air. Though there was no threat of snow, the December air gave Henry and Silas shivers whenever they stopped long enough for the night breeze to cool their wet clothes, their exposed arms chilled in the cold.

"Look there, in the window," Henry said as he pointed to a lone lantern. The boys sprinted towards the house, careful to remain as hunched and quiet as they could manage. They kept vigilant, remaining alert of all potential threats despite their exhaustion. Once they had reached the stoop, they looked to one another in concerned expectation. One of them would have to knock. Summoning the courage for them both, Silas raised his fist, striking the door.

He knocked in the pattern Mr. Herbert had shared with them while in town. One, two, [pause], one, two, three. With each strike, their nerves wound more tightly than the moment before. Worse than knocking were the prolonged seconds waiting for an answer. It felt like an eternity, but eventually, the door cracked open. Revealing an inch of the other side, the boys saw a pair of eyes glaring back at them behind a hollow shotgun muzzle.

"You boys lost?" asked the set of eyes, the voice gruff and broken with age.

"We're looking for the station, sir," Silas said, emphasizing the last word. Not breaking eye contact, refusing to let his fear show.

The eyes blinked slowly, taking time to measure the situation, examining the boys. "Well, I suppose you found it then." The door slowly opened to reveal an older gentleman, bearded with wisps of silver hair atop his head. He lowered the gun quickly, waving them in. "Inside, now."

The boys entered briskly and heard the door shut behind them, locking. Inside the home they found a quaint room illuminated by a handful of lanterns and candles. A woman stepped into the room to see what the noise was.

The man rested his gun in the corner. "Let's get you boys into some dry clothes at least. Ellen, would you mind fixing something for them to eat, I'd imagine they're famished."

The boys changed clothes and sat by the wood stove, feeling warmer than they had in weeks. As the three sat across one another in the kitchen, the boys were unsure how to best thank the man for his kindness.

"Where you two running from?" asked the man.

Henry answered softly, not maintaining eye contact for very long. "We left one of those corn farms out west."

"Of course. I'd imagine you were about to get the land ready for planting come January. Never mind that now. Looking for your freedom, I suppose. You're fortunate to be doing it now instead of earlier like some. All you really need to do now is to get away from Texas."

The boys furrowed their brows in slight confusion as the man reached towards the counter, retrieving a piece of paper. He began unfolding it, sliding forks and glasses out of the way to lay it flat on the table. He placed his finger on a point. "We are here. Your best bet," he traced a penciled line, "is to follow this route northwards. You're aiming for Kansas, since Oklahoma can still be hit or miss. At least they recognize the law."

"Sir, I'm afraid we're a bit lost. What law? What were you saying about Texas?" Silas asked.

The man searched their eyes, recognizing their ignorance. He should have known that they would be unaware, but this fact had escaped him for the briefest moment. He looked at his hands, unable to face them when he broke the news. "A few years back, they made it against the law to own slaves. They gave you your freedom."

He snuck a glance and saw their confused, fearful expressions before continuing. "Some states refused, and Texas was chief among them. Now, it is one in a handful that isn't giving these freedoms. That's why I was suggesting you get out of Texas." He finally looked at them to search their expressions, their eyes wide and unfocused as they tried to understand the injustice.

Quietly, painfully, Henry asked, "So you're saying we're supposed to be free, but we're not because we live in Texas?"

"That about sums it up, yes."

Silas clenched his eyes closed, his face shifting upwards towards the sky that he could not see in this small shack.

Henry whispered again. "But we can't leave Texas yet."

It was the old man's turn for surprise. "Why not? Why come to me if you're not planning to leave?"

Silas turned to Henry, ignoring the old man's questions. "You have to go without me."

Henry shook his head in protest. "I'm not leaving you. You

saved me, it's my turn to return the favor."

The old man tapped his hand on the table. "Boys, mind filling me in here?"

Henry hesitated as he looked at Silas, who said nothing. "We're trying to find his mother before we get out of here."

The old man furrowed his brow, by now very familiar with the story he'd heard from many guests. Everyone wanted to find their loved ones. "Boys, this is hard for me to tell you, but that's what most people want. It doesn't have a happy ending. They usually don't find their loved ones, and if they do, the chances of everyone making it out safely are slim. The best chance for your survival is to get out as fast as you can. I'm sure you're already being searched for."

"I know where she is, I just have to get her out," Silas said solemnly.

"Please, I'm begging you both: get out of Texas. Come morning, head straight for Kansas and don't look back."

"Sir, we appreciate your help. You've been kinder than anyone has been to us in ages. But I must do this," Silas said firmly.

"And he's not going alone, either," Henry added.

The old man stared hard into Silas' eyes for a brief moment, recognizing the resolution of spirit. "Alright then. Can either of you read?"

Silas looked at him, perplexed by the question. "I can a little. Henry?"

Henry shook his head. "Not too well, no."

"How about your mother?" asked the old man.

Silas' eyes creased with his smile. "Yes sir, she can. She's the one who showed me."

The old man stood, taking a page from a stack of loose papers that sat on a nearby shelf. Printed across the top was the title,

"Dwight's Journal of Music". "I want you to take this with you and share it often. Share it with your mother. I don't have much to offer, but this is the best Christmas blessing I can give."

Silas took the page, scrunching his face as he held it close to his eyes. He laboriously tried to read the words of the title. Slowly, he read aloud, "*O Holy Night.*"

"It's a song that's gotten real popular recently. Comes from a magazine. I think the last verse is what you'd find most interesting."

Silas looked at the old man, touched. He handed the page back. "Would you show us how it goes?"

The old man took the page gently. "Of course, of course." He cleared his throat, mindful of the two visitors listening intently. He began with the third verse, anxious to see the expression on the two faces before him. When he arrived at the lines about breaking chains, slaves and brothers, he saw them look at one another. Their expressions carried excitement and wonder, as if fueled by the words. Their wonder lasted the entire duration of the song.

Once he had finished singing, the old man returned the page to Silas. Silas took it and pressed it to his chest. Looking to the old man, he expressed his thanks with a handshake. The boys went to bed that night, waking just before the sun peaked the horizon. They continued their journey, together, in search of lost family and the freedom they desperately longed for.

Movement II: Adagio

Boston 1855

John Sullivan Dwight awoke suddenly as he heard the clicking of locks, signifying the arrival of others to the office. His legs were inclined, resting on the edge of the couch in his office while the rest of his body lay sorely on the floor, surrounded by pages of music. He rubbed his face to awaken as he squinted his eyes towards the clock. Groggily deciphering the mess around him, faint memories of the early morning hours returning to him. He remembered translating the lyrics, deciding to rest his eyes for a moment before attaching them to the music. Very well, he must have needed the rest.

First sitting up, then rising to his feet, John's eyes examined the pages that were strewn across the room. He saw junk mixed in with the newly discarded notes and drafts of the poem. He remembered laying the finished words on his desk, but where was the music? He crouched down, digging through the mess. As he had located it, he heard the door to his office open quietly.

"Good morning, Harriet."

Harriet's eyes scanned from John to the clutter around him, stopping as she noticed the sheet in his hand. "Find what you were looking for?" Her eyes attempted to mask the concern she had for John.

He smirked. "I did, thanks. Yesterday I received a song to translate that may be the best thing I've ever gotten to work on. Stayed up all night, and I'm about to add it to its music. But I'm worried I can't publish it. Can I ask a favor?"

Harriet stepped into the office, closing the door. "Of course sir, what is it?"

John stood, walking to his desk. "Give me an hour to finish this. Then, come back to hear it. I need an honest set of ears and your opinion has always been helpful to me." As Harriet turned to leave, John gave one last request. "And please, tell no one about this." Harriet exited.

In the following hour, John worked rigorously, propelled by a wonder that he had long forgotten was within himself. He merged the translated lyrics to the music, making the necessary changes to convey the original spirit of the piece. He then moved on to smoothing his playing, so much so that by the hour's end he had played through twice in full confidence.

When Harriett returned to the office, reserved excitement carried her. "Is it ready?" she asked.

John had already positioned a chair for her beside the piano. "I believe so. Have a seat." Harriet did so.

John positioned his hands over the keys, hesitating for one moment as reverence found him. "As far as I'm aware, this is the first time this piece has been played in English. It has been removed from worship in its own country of France. I'm afraid what this might do to our Journal if it's published. But I can't imagine not sharing it." After one final pause, John began to play.

His fingers glided from note to note triumphantly as his voice gently sang the translated words, the lyrics and music blending beautifully together in complementary union. To Harriet's surprise, John was playing with his eyes closed, obviously entranced by the piece. He must have the lyrics written on his soul, she thought. Had he missed any notes? There was no way to know. But something about the perfection made her think it was unimaginable he had.

When he finished, opening his eyes as his hum trailed off, he turned to look at Harriet expectantly. Her hand clutched a handkerchief which she had pressed to her mouth, hiding her expression. But her eyes told him enough. They were open wide, glossed with moisture. John patiently waited for her to say something. Finally she said shakily, "They need to hear this."

John didn't understand who she was referring to. "Ok, I'll take it to the editors' meeting this afternoon to get their thoughts."

Harriet shook her head, waving his words aside with the handkerchief. "No, not them. The country needs to hear this. This is what Christmas is about, what our churches are about. Humility. Surrender. The grace of God. All of it. They need to hear it."

John sat back, surprised by the strong assessment. "So you think I should move forward with it?"

Harriet leaned towards him, staring him squarely in the eyes. "Not only do I think it should be published, but I think now that you've translated it, it is your responsibility to get this into our world. Not everyone is going to welcome it, but you've got to make them hear it."

...

Harriet had been right about opposition, but John hadn't expected it so soon. For a translation that had existed for a mere fifteen hours, the court of opinion was already having a field day with it. He had presented it at the editors meeting, giving everyone a copy of the score as he played for them. He didn't even get to finish the third verse before their uproar stopped him.

"John, you know better than anyone what this will do to our sales. It's been over two quarters since that other piece and we have finally recovered readership. This isn't the time for more statements," said Gerald. The editors sat at the conference table, John separated from them by the piano bench.

John tried to appeal. "Our readers appreciate our boldness, our taste. We are the foremost voice in music publication, shouldn't we feel obligated to challenge the boundaries of our listeners, encouraging them to push their own?"

Alexander spoke this time. "John, I don't think it wise for us to publish songs of criticism right now. I can only imagine how the Catholic Church would react to this. Plus, the slavery angle throws us at an entirely different beast altogether."

"Alexander, we can't be scared, lukewarm."

"That's not what this is about."

John slammed the lid over the keys, demanding everyone's attention. "This is one of the best songs we've ever had the chance to promote. Does anyone disagree?" All were silent. "This song needs to be heard. I feel a responsibility here. And I believe in our readers to understand and cherish it for what it is: the reminder we all need this Christmas."

The editors examined him quietly, not giving any indication of where their sentiments were. Alexander spoke softly, everyone turned to him. "You've always told us that though this paper bears your name on the front, it bears our imprints too, so we need to be happy with the contents. I think we should take a vote." His last sentence, though even and soft, carried what John believed to be a challenge.

He deftly shook his head in agreement. "Alright, let's vote then."

"Those in favor, raise a hand." John and two others raised their hands, each scanning the room, hoping to have seen more. With a smirk, Alexander said "Those opposed?" The rest raised their hands, seven in total. Their expressions varying from apologetic to angry. No one said a word. Alexander assumed an expression of false sorrow. "I'm sorry. You just don't have the votes."

John sat quietly for the remainder of the meeting, not leaving the piano bench, not listening to the rest of the meeting. Once the meeting wrapped, Alexander adjourned it. After everyone had left the room, he turned to the piano once more, finishing the third verse, the verse that had been interrupted. What did they not hear? he wondered. Despite the nearly unanimous objection, he still found that his belief in the song compelled him onward. He exited the conference room. Instead of turning left to his office, he turned right. He needed to pay the copy printers a visit.

Boston 2005

After two weeks of rehearsals following the disastrous introduction of Hall, Bryn entered Charles' office. His desperation outshone any pleasantries. "We need to talk," he said. Charles, seated at his desk, had been reviewing the final drafts of some marketing material as Bryn spoke. The intrusion hadn't surprised him, knowing it was only a matter of time. He gave Bryn a friendly welcome, encouraging him to take a seat but Bryn continued to stand.

"What about?" Charles asked, looking upward to Bryn.

"Some of the musicians have expressed their concerns with him. His attitude and the way he belittles everyone is unacceptable."

"I see. And do you share their concerns?" Charles asked expectantly.

Bryn had been wringing his hands as he paced short, sharp two-step paths. He hesitated to answer. "Yes, I do. He's always late. He treats everyone as inferior, including me. Just last rehearsal he suggested to me that I not conduct the song, that the musicians could just follow his lead. He still leaves early, too! I'm not sure we've gotten to run the song more than once all the way through with him." Bryn paused finally, taking a breath. He shook his head, speaking slower. "He's tried to change the lyrics again. I'm afraid he's going to do it during the actual show. That is, if he stays for it."

Charles put down the card-stock, shifting his entire focus to Bryn. His expression was gentle as he addressed him. "Please, have a seat." Bryn sat this time, taking note of Charles' concern.

A silence hung between them, except for the small sounds of their breathing. Charles spoke again. "He's being difficult. How are the musicians reacting? Has it hurt morale?"

Bryn continued passionately, "They were obviously stressed before Hall came along. The timeline from rehearsals to performance was pushing it, but they knew that. The last thing they need is some 'celebrity' draining their energy and distracting them from the art. And, he's directly disrupting their work, which I can tell is frustrating them."

Charles listened attentively. He quietly asked, "How would you deal with Hall if he were one of the musicians? A cellist or a woodwind?"

Bryn thought for a second. "I'd speak to him directly. I'd remind him he was a part of the whole, and if he couldn't find a way to meet the collective vision, someone else would gladly take his chair."

Charles raised an eyebrow. "Have you tried that with him?"

"He's a little different, don't you think?" Bryn responded, cheeks flushed.

"Yes, but my point is that maybe you should have some version of that conversation with Hall. I know it's not the same, but that could be an effective way to try and get him on board. If it worked, it might help his respect, too. Surely he realizes, deep down, that he needs the orchestra. Be tactful and patient, of course. No shouting this time."

"I'm not sure it would work like you think. If he already doesn't respect what I say, why start now?"

Charles shrugged. "Maybe you're right. But should you choose to give it a try, you have my full support. I mean, it's worth a shot. But it's your call."

Bryn nodded stoically. Charles noticed that he hadn't moved towards getting up and leaving, his eyes glazed over as he stared, lost in thought.

"Is there something else on your mind?" Charles asked, unsure.

Bryn's lips parted once or twice to speak, then closed again. He eventually found some words to express his conflict. "Is it even any good?"

Charles didn't answer, not sure what he was asking, so Bryn went on. "I mean, I just want to do it justice. It needs to be powerful and reverent. I'm not sure that's what my arrangement is."

Charles was surprised by the lack of confidence. Bryn was no stranger to anxieties and doubt, but not in his composition. That was where he always had found his confidence. Maybe that was the source of his recent troubles. "The arrangement is beautiful, Bryn. Everyone I talk to thinks so. It's impressive and grand, what's more appropriate for the anniversary?"

"That's just it. I don't think it needs to be grand or impressive. I fear I let myself be tempted with what it could be instead of focusing on what it should be. Have I let the music stray too far? This piece was originally written and performed with a new organ, a vocalist, and a small choir. When it came to the States, people were satisfied performing it acapella while caroling. Meanwhile, I've got musicians performing instrumental acrobatics three times over. The beauty has always been in its simplicity. Everyone knows that. Everyone but me, perhaps."

"What are you saying?" Charles hoped he was concealing his rising concern.

"I'm saying that I might have made a big mistake, and I'm afraid to see the consequences."

They sat in silence for some time. Bryn continued to stare into space. Charles placed his fingertips together in thought. Eventually, he spoke. "Change the charts."

Bryn's eyes widened, as if he hadn't considered the idea of such an insane action. "The show is in a week. There's no way."

"Sounds to me like you've got a whole week to make some magic happen," Charles said, amused. In his experience, Bryn's best work had manifested from a combination of two things: deadlines and artistic drive. Charles could only give one. He prayed Bryn might be feeling the other.

"But that's not fair to the musicians. Even if in some absurd world it were possible, I'd have to write something first!" Bryn was floundering. But Charles had an instinct about his friend; an instinct that he could pull this off. He just needed the right nudge.

"I mean, it's up to you. But I know what you're capable of. I also know how meaningful your music can be when you fully believe in what you wrote. Don't be afraid to take a risk. Make something you're proud of; especially if the alternative is performing something you're not."

Bryn's mind raced, gears spinning in overdrive. Charles examined his watch, casually adding, "I don't mean to kick you out, but you'll probably be late for rehearsal if you don't leave now."

Bryn shook his head, reality returning to focus. He stood,

turning to leave the office. At the doorway, he paused, turning his head. "Thank you, Charles. I mean it. Thank you."

"Hey, what are friends for?"

Roquemaure 1847

Placide Cappeau roused himself after the third round of knocks clanked against his front door. His sense of urgency overcame the brief confusion that ran through his mind as he tried to wake fully. He shuffled cautiously down the dark hallway. "I'm coming, I'm coming, settle down", he said hoarsely. He fumbled in lighting the lamp, knowing the street outside would not offer any help. When he finally managed to keep his strike ablaze, he shuffled to the door and opened it. He found Adolphe Adam's eyes blazing brighter than the wick as he slipped inside.

"I must show you something, I've been working all night. Get dressed, we're going to the cafe," Adolphe commanded.

Placide examined his friend's face worriedly. "Adolphe, are you alright? It's the middle of the night."

Adolphe glanced at the watch he had in his pocket. "It's morning technically. The beginning of a new day. Now get dressed, I've already asked Albert to unlock the place for us."

Placide rubbed his eyes. "You woke Albert for this? Poor man. Couldn't this wait 'til morning?"

Adolphe stepped closer to Placide, staring at him with a wildness in his eyes. "Placide, if you don't get dressed in the next two minutes, I'm going to drag you down the street in your nightgown. Go!"

Placide turned quickly, obeying the command. He slipped into the clothes he had worn the day previous, not taking the time to ensure his shirt was properly tucked or that his buttons were correctly aligned. He rushed to satisfy Adolphe.

He briskly walked back to the foyer where Adolphe waited. Without a word, Adolphe opened the door and set off down the street, not taking a second to wait. The two men hurried to their favorite cafe. "Please, won't you tell me what's going on?" Placide asked, trailing Adolphe.

Adolphe glanced back, smiling a ravaged grin. "I have it, dear friend. Our song found its wings."

…

As the pair entered the empty cafe, the wooden door creaking, their eyes adjusted to the dimly lit hall. Albert had lit a handful of lanterns for them and prepared a small table by the piano. He had placed two mugs next to an uncorked bottle, but neither paid them any mind, more enthralled by the song.

Adolphe took his seat on the piano bench as Placide dragged a chair from the table to sit closer. As Adolphe shifted his body on the bench, settling into the seat, he retrieved some pages from a folder he'd been carrying. Among the pages was the poem Placide had let him borrow, now riddled with a generous amount of notes and revisions. He lifted the wood that had covered the keys, allowing his fingers to brush them without pressing. With a deep inhalation and slow exhalation, Adolphe's shoulders relaxed. He turned to Placide, "I just couldn't help myself. It demanded to be heard."

In a voice that distantly sounded not unlike his own, Placide responded, "I know." Adolphe began to play, his fingers dancing across the keys in the fluid arpeggio that he'd alluded to before. He played it in cycle, adding nuanced changes with each repetition. After fully completing the sequence, his chin slightly raised as he began to sing.

O Holy Night,
the stars are brightly shining
it is the night of our dear savior's birth

Placide could already see a tonal change from what he'd written, but it didn't bother him; the heart was the same. He grew curious, his concern from days before not quelling. These sentiments would still likely be hard for Père Gilles to hear, or accept. But the savior's birth was still at the forefront. The guiding light of the thing was still shining as a beacon to strive towards.

Long lay the world
in sin and error pining
till He appeared, and the soul felt its worth

Placide wondered where Adolphe had found such words, their beauty foreign against those of his own composition. Where he had toiled with wrath, Adolphe had found a way to bring hope and peace to the work. Even the most broken souls seek this place of worth and value.

A thrill of hope,
the weary world rejoices
for yonder braes a
new and glorious morning.

But Adolphe had kept the complexity of our sinful existence, and Placide was astounded by his ability to do so in such an effortless and direct way. How had he kept our sinfulness in the lens while keeping the Divinity as the focal point?

Fall to your knees
O hear the angel voices
O night, divine, O night
when Christ was born

Yes! The surrender! The humility! Confession in the highest regard. Placide listened as Adolphe played the composition laced with sentiments that his optimism could have only dreamed. He sang earnestly, words of broken chains, enslaved brothers, and the supreme power of the born Christ. Adolphe had taken his fragments and had packaged them well.

After Adolphe had completed the final build of the chorus, his voice still as the last ring of piano died off, they sat silently. They were both keenly aware of the history they had witnessed in that moment, afraid to cut it short. Unable to contain himself any longer, Placide placed his hand gently on Adolphe's shoulder. "It's beautiful, Adolphe."

Adolphe nodded. Placide sat back in his chair. "What now? What do we do with it?"

Adolphe turned on the bench to face Placide. He avoided Placide's eyes, speaking tentatively. "I think we take it to Père Gilles. His request started this whole thing, though I doubt he envisioned this."

"I don't know if I can do that. This isn't what he wanted, and I still don't think I can be a part of the commemoration. I can't be there with everyone, or Gilles. Not after how I left. They probably wouldn't understand the piece anyway."

Adolphe spoke calmly, despite his directness. "You still have a low view of them, don't you?"

Placide's cheeks grew warm with embarrassment. "What would you have of me? To forget the sin and hypocrisy, to forgive the unkindness?"

"Would that be so terrible?" Adolphe sat forward slightly, "Can I challenge you? Do you not believe that we are all sinful, needing the redemption everyone in that church seeks?"

Placide did not answer, averting his glance to the untouched mug on the table before him.

Adolphe continued, careful to keep his tone free of the sharpness it was prone to. "I'll assume you do believe that, considering this poem you wrote. So tell me; if we are all desperately in need of redemption, why do you still expect them to be perfect? And why judge those seeking Christ more harshly than others when they fall short? Feels a touch absurd, honestly."

Placide spoke softly, his mouth dry from the tension. "Anything else?"

"Yes, actually. It bothers me how terribly you oppose and demean Père Gilles when all he tries to do is to reconcile with you, despite the arguments and differences. I mean, I have love for you, but sometimes even I can't believe he's still trying." Adolphe stopped, rubbing the back of his head thoughtlessly. "I don't know why your answer to the church member's attitudes and your differences with Mon Père was to run away from everything. Why abandon worship when your issue was with the people, not God? It felt disappointingly lazy."

The room sat, swallowed in a silence that both men were afraid to tamper with. Adolphe glanced at Placide, but could not read his expression. Eventually, he spoke again. "I'm sorry, Placide. That was harsh. I shouldn't have brought it up. Not now.

Placide paused, searching for his voice. "It's quite alright. Speak your mind, friend." He stood, crossing to the piano to examine the music more closely. His eyes squinted as took in the composition. He placed a hand on Adolphe's shoulder. "This piece is the best part of us both. It should be heard, and I think it can reveal the best in others, too. Let's take it to Mon Père."

Boston 1855

John Sullivan Dwight jumped as the office door shot open, forcefully striking the wall. The contact had made a frame fall from the wall, but the man behind it paid no attention to the crash. Looking up, John saw Alexander storming into his office, followed by a handful of red-faced editors. John barely had enough time to recognize the magazine that was hurled at him, hitting him squarely in the chest.

"What is this?" Alexander shouted, pointing towards the magazine.

"Can we take a second to calm…"

"No, calm has passed. You ignored our vote and went around the editors in order to publish that piece."

Trying to maintain composure, John hurriedly flipped through the pages to find his translator's note. He held it up. "If you'll notice, I also added a disclosure accepting full responsibility for the piece. I distanced anyone other than myself from whatever happened. I feel terrible about how this whole thing has transpired, I'm sorry. But this song will outlive us all. I'm certain of this, please try to see that."

Alexander shook his head in frustration. "No one claimed it was a bad song, or even questioned its importance. We were being responsible to the publication above ourselves. Not all of us have the financial cushion of the great John Sullivan Dwight. We want to still have jobs after this issue!" Alexander stepped closer to John, threateningly. "We all voted. But you refused to accept that and did what you wanted. Our voices mean nothing, why are we here?"

John had no answer for him. He felt the shame growing. "I accept full responsibility for the outcome. But can we please not react too harshly until we see the results? Let's see what the sales reports look like."

Without answering, the group stormed out of John's office. He looked to the open pages before him, this tumultuous situation of his own creation sending his thoughts running. He had betrayed the editor's trust, and now feared that it may have all been in vain.

As John sat at his desk, brow furrowed, Harriet entered quietly. "John, do you have a moment?"

"I'm sorry, I don't think this is the best time."

"John, I just wanted to tell you that I got my copy of the Journal at the newsstand this morning. It was a very moving issue."

John did not look at her. "Thank you."

She lingered, more to say. "I was running a little late, so I got there close to eight instead of my usual seven-thirty."

John looked at her curiously, not sure what she was getting at. A proud grin found her. "I got the last issue. They'd sold out."

· · ·

John still fretted over the arrival of the sales reports as the moments passed. Part of him oddly hoped for poor numbers. That way, it would be easier to tuck his tail and apologize, definitive proof that he had done the wrong thing. Being wrong would be so much easier. But if he was right, well, he would address that later.

"The reports have arrived," John said, trying to maintain a neutral and natural tone as he entered the meeting. He passed them around. Each editor dove into the report, searching for answers as it came to them. The blank, curious faces quickly changed to those of surprise, excitement, and even dread. Alexander finished the quickest, sliding it slowly away from him. He stared defiantly at the wall in front of him.

"Gentlemen, it was never my aim to overrule your judgment or silence your voice. I felt we were on the wrong path, but the way I responded to that showed worse judgment. I'm sorry. This success, though grand, does not excuse my actions or serve as an example." John's voice was soft with concern.

No one replied to his apology. The editors merely glanced at one another uncomprehendingly. Finally, Alexander stood and shuffled around the conference table to John. Without a word, he removed a folded piece of paper and tossed it unconcernedly on the table in front of John. His eyes lingered a brief second, conveying both his distaste and his resolve in a pained wordlessness. Turning his back to John, he left the conference room.

John stared at the paper before him, almost certain of its contents. He felt each eye in the room staring at him. He leaned forward and opened it. The few short lines confirmed his expectation. Though professional, it was a statement of resignation from Alexander, citing creative difference and loss of supervisory trust. What stung more than anything was how easily John understood the decision. Without mentioning the contents of the letter, he addressed the room. "As you see, sales are the strongest we have ever seen for a single issue. We're already printing more to restock our merchants. I ran some inquiries as to what caused such a demand and I'm told that quite a few recreational singing groups purchased copies in bulk to perform the piece."

Otto spoke up for the first time. "I'd heard that too, mainly because my wife is in a choir that wanted to do so. They asked me to get them some copies since they had sold out everywhere." The editors murmured at such a closely related confirmation of the news. Otto continued, "It gave me an idea, if I may. I ran some calculations under the assumption that we had sold out in most places and we have more than enough margin to do it." He paused, embarrassed by what he hadn't even proposed yet.

John encouraged him, excited to hear the idea. "Go ahead, what is it?"

Otto nervously looked around before locking on John's eyes for comfort. "Well, what if we printed a large lot of just the sheet music of the song? Then, we get the word out that any group that wants copies to perform, we'll send them free of charge. Call it a Christmas gift."

Another editor chimed in next, adding to the idea. "I know some people over at other publications. What if we asked them to pitch in, too? Maybe run a small advertisement in their publications about the sheet music."

John was impressed by how quickly the editors had adapted to Alexander's absence, jumping to further the vision of what had become. "I think those are fantastic ideas, men. Objections?" As he looked around, the other editors murmured in approval, each assuming a lighter attitude than they had before. Smiling, he clapped his hands together excitedly. "Perfect, then let's get to it."

Iraq 2004

Chaplain Michaels,

I apologize for my delay in writing you. If I'm honest with myself, each time I sat down, I either found myself discouraged by the lack of progress or disheartened by my own faith's failings. The past few months have been trying, not that I should have expected anything else. No matter what you told me, nothing could have prepared me to minister to these young men, in a foreign, hostile land no less. I've been in Fallujah for two and a half months and I fear I keep finding myself aching to come home. Come to think of it, I'm not even sure that it's the distance or the war zone that makes me feel this way. I think it is mainly because this is my first infirmary assignment, and these men are in a bad state. Worst of all, their burdens are all direct results of the actions of other men, whose sole intent is to bring them pain. I had not considered this when I volunteered.

Sometimes, I find my duties hard to carry out, I'm ashamed to admit. I know and believe in God's promise for us all; I preach it to the men. I assure them of His protective hand, the hope that trusting in Him should bring. But in their eyes I see the wear that their souls have endured, the callousness that they have had no choice but to adopt. When I tell them of this hope, they rarely listen. And what can I do? The worst fears in the men's imagination have now become their reality.

I've adjusted my usual approach in speaking to these soldiers. I hadn't realized how much I'd been relying on the scripts I'd made for myself instead of actual thought. I tried first to relate to the struggles of the soldiers, but they were able to see through my inexperience instantly. I tried to relate their struggles to that of the Israelite's, but it was too abstract and fell flat. I shifted to Job, rather tactlessly, and still found no success. Many were discouraged to hear the great lengths he suffered while still being a man of God.

Unfortunately, my embarrassments didn't stop. I've had some unfortunate encounters while performing some of the ceremonial duties. One of my first weeks here, trying to fill the silence with a soldier, I asked if I could take his confession. I knew my mistake as soon as I asked, but that didn't stop him from responding. "Well, I shot a man last week," he said to me loudly. "And if you don't get out of here, I might shoot another." I left.

That same week, I caught myself extending the cup of the sacrament to a man who had just lost his hand. I quickly caught the error, but not before it was noticed by him. I even tried to administer them to a soldier whose mouth was bandaged closed. By my fourth week here, I was too afraid to perform my duties that I only felt comfortable praying with the soldiers. But none of this is why I finally write to you. Honestly, I had reached the point where I was so ashamed of myself that I'd resigned to taking whatever reprimand came from not contacting you instead of divulging my failures. But then I met Private Daniels.

I found myself by Daniels' bed the same way I found others:

through mere luck or misfortune. Regardless, there I was, seated in a chair next to his bed at eleven on a Sunday, trying to convince him to attend one of our services. I'd been informed he was religious, though I knew not what denomination, and that he might welcome a visitor. I'm not sure where that idea came from because Daniels didn't acknowledge me when I entered his room, or when I greeted him. Instead, his eyes remained unfocused, facing the sky outside his second floor window.

Daniels is young. Probably in his first deployment, a shame for it to result in the injury he sustained. Sometimes when I enter a room, it is difficult to know exactly what ails the soldiers. Sometimes they have inconspicuously small bandages, or no visible bandages at all. Some are mobile and active, while others are so heavily bandaged and sedated, it would be easier to assume what didn't ail them. But in Daniels' case, fewer assumptions were needed, for at the end of his bed, there was only one peak of the blanket that covered his lone foot.

I tried to get him to answer, or at least acknowledge I was there. I offered to read him some passages or pray with him. I even offered to sit quietly with him for a spell, eager to take a seat after leading mass and visiting rooms for a while. But no answer came. Instead, the quiet was filled with the rattle and hum of the wall unit along with the occasional squeak of a sneaker on the floor outside or rhythmic beep of monitors down the hall. After waiting long enough to be sure that he would not speak, I dismissed myself. I almost made it out the door when I heard his youthful, broken voice speak. "What do you think it was, Father? Wasn't I faithful enough?"

Obviously, the question caught me off-guard. I'm used to arguing, berating, and the regular nonbeliever, but Daniels struck me with the tone in which his question was delivered.

He wasn't hateful or loud. He was quiet. He was earnest for an answer, because the suffering he'd faced didn't reconcile with the faith he thought he had displayed his whole life. I stepped back into the room. "I'm not sure what you mean," I said, trying to be careful.

"Maybe it was my father's sins, or his father's, or even further back." His pained voice carried the entire weight of his world, begging for assurance, answers. I'm sad to say I didn't know how to give him anything at that moment. Not then. Instead, I think I wrung my hands, probably avoiding his gaze.

"During my mission, I prayed routinely, studied routinely, attended mass, and took the sacrament. I've served Him as well as I could imagine, or so I thought," Daniels said.

"I'm sorry for your pain, Daniels, but I can assure you that this suffering has nothing to do with your faithfulness. You're not being punished. Not even Jesus himself was without suffering, and he was the most righteous of all." I was glad to have answered him but also dissatisfied with the quality of it. I know what you'd say; that I should have pressed him further, comforted him more instead of sending generic, stock answers back to him.

But alas, I didn't, and he noticed. Daniels sank into his bed, head leaning back on his pillow as his eyes fixed upward. They had a thin covering of moisture. "Being here, in this place…" he began. He struggled in search of his words. "I feel so desolate and alone. I'm not with my family, or my company." He closed his eyes tightly. "I don't even know if anyone else survived."

I sat with him silently, afraid to engage, and he was seemingly too occupied in his own thoughts. We sat for nearly ten minutes before another word was uttered. Eventually, the young private sat up as if startled and looked at me. "What day is it, Father?

Please tell me, am I to be alone on Christmas, too?"

"It's December 19th, a Sunday. Still some time before Christmas," I answered.

His head returned to his pillow. "Just the same, I doubt I'll leave this place before then."

I wanted to comfort him, wanted to assure him that an entire life waited just on the other side of this hospital stay. I wanted to enrich his faith, but all my words felt cosmetic and dull, no depth or action held in them. I was rescued from my unpursued efforts when a knock came to the door. We both looked to see the origin of the sound and were greeted by a group of nearly ten men and women in uniforms accessorized by Santa hats and the like, each holding black folios with gold lettering on the fronts.

"Merry Christmas!" said the woman closest. She looked at me and then at Daniels. "We're making the rounds this afternoon to spread some cheer and sing some carols. Thought a mood booster may be part of the Doctor's orders."

Daniels groaned. "A carol is the last thing…"

"What about *O Holy Night*?" I said, cutting Daniels off. "I know, predictable, but also a classic." The group nodded, opening their folios to find it. I added as an afterthought, "and if you have the second verse, I'd especially love to hear that part." They smiled and nodded in understanding.

The singers arranged themselves in a half-circle as they found the correct page and the woman removed a small silver disc from her pocket, blowing into it to play their starting key. A few of the members hummed it back quietly, each nodding to her. She then raised her arm, every member taking a collective breath as they began.

They sang beautifully. Better than my attempts at leading

singing at Mass. Their voices blended well, each expressing the holiday spirit they tried to spread. I shifted my glance to Daniels, unsure if he was enjoying the song as much as I was. He sat unmoved, eyes fixed elsewhere. When they began the second verse, I listened more attentively, knowing the words I wanted to hear. They sang the lyrics; words of gratitude, faith, and glowing hearts. They sang of the coming wise men. *In all our trials, born to be our friend*, they sang gladly. It was at that line that I saw Daniels' head move slightly: he was hearing them.

They continued, *He knows our needs, to our weakness is no stranger*. Daniels closed his eyes. At first, I thought he was again trying to tune them out. But without expression or words, I felt Daniels take my hand in his. A thin trail of tears fell as his eyes found mine. He nodded, as if offering his thanks.

There was no great revelation, no great life turn. But the assurances of Jesus were able to comfort the upended soul of this young man, riddled by the unknown. We each found the company of fraternity, the invocation of our souls resting in their intended space. And where I came up short in my service to God, He still intervened to bring comfort. I hope it brought some type of rejuvenation to Daniels, because it did to me.

I thank you for your continued letters and prayers. I wish you a Merry Christmas.

In thankfulness for our Savior's birth,

Chaplain Andrews

Movement III: Minuet

Boston 1856

One year following the publication of *O Holy Night* in Dwight's Journal of Music, readership had increased substantially, necessitating the addition of more members to their staff. The usual hustle and bustle had given way to the mounting pressure they had grown to feel: how would they follow the previous year's success? As John's team worked diligently to meet the holiday deadline, he found himself proud of the issue they'd delivered. He took comfort in everyone's passion and for the quality of the contents of the pages.

As the afternoon slipped slowly into early evening, the staff was trickling out in the fallen snow; Harriet entered John's office. "Do you have a moment to spare? We have some carolers ready to sing some tunes for us out front."

John removed his glasses, placing them on the pages of the proof he had been reviewing. "I'm not sure, I'm trying to get this wrapped up before I head home."

Harriet smirked, assuming a lighter tone. "Otto said I'm not to take no for an answer, sir."

John sat up, curious to know what Otto could be getting at. "Well, if Otto insists, who am I to say no?" He stood, grabbing his coat from the hook by his door. He followed Harriet down the hall to the front desk where he saw the Journal's staff gathered around a dozen carolers. Each caroler had a small booklet of music that he quickly recognized as their own publication from last year. As he scanned the faces of the singers, his eyes stopped suddenly as they caught sight of Alexander standing among the carolers.

As the leader hummed a note and signaled the beginning of the piece, John and Alexander stared at one another. Each saw traces of the bitterness that had wedged between them. But by the first chorus, as everyone sang the special words, their eyes shone the humility and then forgiveness that each would have been too proud to say aloud. In their melodies, filling the halls of the Journal, John and Alexander allowed it to enter the broken space in their hearts, filling the gaps to make them whole again.

Boston 2005

Bryn rubbed the bridge of his nose, his eyes clenched tightly as he tried to disassociate for a moment. His mind raced from the suggestions Charles made for changes to the charts. He considered talking to Hall before rehearsal, but Hall had predictably arrived late, along with much more persistence than usual.

"I mean, don't be stupid, Ben…"

"His name's Bryn, idiot," said a trumpeter.

Hall turned to the musician. "I think you should adjust your attitude. No offense, but there's a reason I'm known by name and you are only a member of the band. My experience may do you well."

As Hall walked back from speaking to the musician, the trumpeter timed his spit valve empty for the exact moment he passed, depositing the sludge on Hall's shoe. Not that he noticed, which amused Bryn even more.

Hall continued speaking, actively looking for someone who would listen. The number of those continued to diminish. "I know I keep saying it, but we should update these lyrics and add a more modern sound. Right now, those two minutes of these instruments, it's a bit of a snooze fest."

Another trumpet player stood in objection, Bryn quickly waved him to take his seat. He knew that despite his fatigue and worry, to say nothing of Hall's lunacy, he needed to talk to him today. "Hall, a word." He led Hall to the wings in search of privacy, but knew it was in vain due to Hall's complete lack of awareness.

"What's the word? Ready to make my changes?"

Bryn put his arm firmly around Hall, redirecting his gaze to the orchestra. "Take a look. How many musicians do you see?"

"I don't know, probably 40 or so."

Bryn shook his head emphatically. "There are nearly a hundred. But despite there being nearly a hundred, all doing their own portion, all are working to create one united song. That's what makes the performance so beautiful. So many talented individuals striving to create a singular work of art."

Hall nodded, uninterested. "Cool."

"I can tell it's not something you're used to."

"I mean, I've got a band."

Bryn squinted his eyes. "It's a bit different. But that might be part of the issue. You're viewing all this as backup to you, but that's not the case. Here, everyone is an equal piece. But that's not how you are handling it."

Hall squared up defensively. "Wait a minute, you asked me here to perform. You needed a superstar to add some flair to your show."

Bryn was able to maintain his cool. "It's a shame you were led to believe that. We thought it would be fun to have a popular, well loved singer to help celebrate the historic anniversary of this song." Bryn paused for emphasis. Hall smiled at the perceived compliment, happy to hear Bryn's praise. "But that singer had to back out, so we asked you."

"You better watch it," Hall said, his cheeks flushing. "I could walk away now and leave. You're not going to find a star as big as me to come sing for you."

Summoning the energy that his friend had often used on him in times of distress, Bryn spoke as Charles would have. "Hey, that's totally up to you— if that's what you want. No worries here. But if you don't leave, you're right about one thing. There needs to be some change." Hall's eyes widened in anticipation, and for the first time, fear.

"I need a team player instead of you insisting you are the star of the show. You're not. The first step would be to not refer to yourself as a star ever again. It's just sad. You will show the musicians the respect they deserve. Especially considering how gracious they have been to you through this process. And I would also remind you: I too am a musician."

Hall laughed viciously. "That's rich. Like you'd even sell tickets if my name wasn't top of the bill. Maybe I should go talk to Charles about it, see if he shares your sentiments." He smirked as the threat hung in the air, but faltered when he noticed the amusement on Bryn's face.

"I think that would be a good idea."

Hall blinked, surprised. "You know what, I don't have to listen to this. I'm done for the day." He faced his entourage. "Come on boys, time to go." Turning back to Bryn, speaking with more venom that he had before, "Don't push your luck. I might not come back at all." Without objections, Hall and his group gathered their things loudly and left the performance hall.

The silence left in the wake of the doors closing grew exponentially. Bryn took a slow, deep breath and began to return to the stage. As he did so, a flutist began to clap.

Others joined as the reality of the situation set in. Their applause crescendoed, some even stood, patting him on the back. The remaining rehearsal unfolded beautifully. Bryn was undistracted and the musicians eager to follow his lead.

After he dismissed the musicians and returned to his office, he thought about the specifics of the arrangement. He tried to think of ways the sections could be sliced or altered from their current state without undergoing a complete overhaul. He opened the score at his piano, pencil in hand. His foot bounced anxiously as he struggled to find his spark.

Bryn stood, pacing the space between the piano and desk, struggling to find his starting point. He grabbed blank sheets, scribbling notations on them in attempts to redesign the arrangement. He was still working as the afternoon cleaning crew stopped in his office. A woman knocked and entered slowly, quietly taking the wastebasket to empty. Bryn stood to add another sheet to the can she held. "Sorry, one more."

The cleaning woman glanced down, seeing *O Holy Night* on the page. "Oh, I just love that song. My grandmother used to sing it as our lullaby around Christmas time. Sometimes we would sing it quietly together, just the two of us."

Bryn nodded absently. "That sounds lovely." As the door closed, the silent unease returned. Bryn was intrigued by the idea of a lullaby. He sat at the piano once more to play the piece in the style of a lullaby. As the song progressed in the lullaby style, the pieces of a new arrangement began to fall into place.

Long after the staff and musicians should be home with their families, Charles made a final lap around the building to bid his evening farewells. He noticed the light trickling out of Bryn's office and poked his head in. He found Bryn waving his pencil as a baton, pacing the room mindlessly as he stared at a large, marked-up score. Charles knocked to get his attention. Once Bryn heard the knock, he looked to Charles with an expression of both fear and measured excitement. "I took your advice," Bryn said, trying to contain his excitement. "I found it. I found the song."

Charles' lips split into a wide grin. "Then let's get to work."

Roquemaure 1847

The morning sun had yet to rise or shine its light through the newly-installed windows of the Roquemaure sanctuary. Père Gilles did not often find himself sleepless, especially without reason. He had awoken in the wee hours fully alert, his eyes without drowsiness or heaviness. After making his small bed and dressing in his usual attire, he sat by the fireplace studying the book of Luke in his office, as was his habit this time of year. When the frantic knocks beat the church's doors, he was quick to respond, despite the early hour.

As he opened the door, he greeted the visitors with a drop of his jaw, surprised, followed by an exuberant smile. "Adolphe, Placide, what a pleasant surprise. Please, come in."

"Thank you, Mon Père," Adolphe said as he stepped through the doorway. Placide was more hesitant, attempting to trail invisibly behind Adolphe. He planned to allow Adolphe to do all the talking, not wanting to be in conversation with Père Gilles.

Père Gilles stood in the poorly lit foyer, gazing at the pair. "To what do I owe this pleasure? It's a bit early."

Adolphe stared at his shoe for a moment, finding the words

to explain. "Mon Père, we've been working on something."

Gilles looked between the two excitedly. "You have?"

"We have. But we can't show you here. You might want your coat, it's a touch chilly."

They were an odd crew, walking down the street, bundled in heavy coats with chins tucked in an effort to shelter from the wind. A priest, a musician, and a wine merchant walking in the early pre-dawn morning towards an empty tavern. To his credit, Père Gilles displayed no concern for the appearance of their crew nor the destination, which surprised Placide.

They had left everything as it was to retrieve Père Gilles, the lamps still burning and the music still in the stand above the uncovered keys. The lone chair Placide had placed in front of the piano still sat next to the bench. The trio entered the cafe, shaking the snow from their coats as Adolphe ushered Père Gilles towards the table. "Have a seat, Mon Père. We were both as surprised as you to have worked on the piece, let alone finish it. But something kept latching itself to us, not letting us soon forget it." Adolphe's eyes caught Placide's for a brief moment.

Père Gilles smiled, containing his excitement as best he could. "I had hoped to hear from you. I prayed over it many times. I'll admit, I only expected to hear back from one of you. But both is a blessing indeed."

Again, Adolphe glanced at Placide, only this time, a sliver of concern in his eyes. Père Gilles' words had surprised both men and it was intimidating to think how subversive the song they wrote was compared to the song they believe he expected. Adolphe simply nodded as he sat at the piano bench to play the piece. He felt it best not to preface, letting the piece speak for itself.

Adolphe began to play. He played the words that had spoken

first in Placide's mind and hummed in his own ear. He played the piece that had ignited the fervor he'd held in sharing the Salvation story. The piece had even brought Placide back into the company of Père Gilles, if only for a moment. And as he continued to play the inspired song, he thought of those he missed. Those who had gone before. He thought of his mother most.

As Père Gilles listened to the piece, soaking the words in, he was overwhelmed by a realization of his answered prayer as it manifested before him. To God he was grateful for the beauty of such a rich, invocative answer. The other bishops and officials might see fault with such a piece; its implications had hardly any shroud obscuring their meaning. They'd also not take kindly to the prodigal authors. But he was not pessimistic. Even if these two failed to carry the flame, they still reignited it in others.

Placide was alone with the coldness of his thoughts as Adolphe played. He found himself still concerned with Père Gilles. He wrestled with his own beliefs, not sure how to reconcile the fact that Adolphe's transposition of his words echoed even more piercingly in his heart. But he would not let such fears creep into the open, where Père Gilles or Adolphe could notice them; he didn't trust his own defenses.

Soon, the playing came to a close, the last chord ringing until silence fell. Adolphe turned to face Père Gilles once more, though his eyes did not linger. To his comfort, he discovered in one of the brief glances that Père Gilles had tears and a smile on his face. As a single tear twisted and turned, tracing the edge of his upturned lip, Père Gilles spoke softly. "Boys, it's beautiful. And it will challenge a lot of people, but more importantly, inspire them. Bless you."

Both Adolphe and Placide looked at one another, not even attempting to conceal their shock. Père Gilles continued, "Please, may we use it for the Christmas Mass? What better place for it to be heard? How moving it would be for everyone." He looked hopefully between the two. "I'm sure you have an arrangement in mind, Adolphe. The organ, no?"

Adolphe cleared his throat. "Yes, of course. And maybe a choir. With a featured vocalist. I actually have a friend who I think could do it wonderfully."

"Perfect! Would you please ask them?"

"Hold on, we haven't agreed to do it," Placide said grumpily.

Adolphe glanced at Placide, pleading for peace with his eyes. "You said it yourself, people need to hear this, and Père Gilles even agrees, despite your concerns." Père Gilles looked nervously between the two, feeling the tension forming. Adolphe addressed him directly. "Mon Père, we would love to do it."

"Only if you both agree, of course. I do think it will be remembered for years to come." He glanced around the room and made an effort to excuse himself. "I'd better leave you two to discuss it further. Just know that the church would love to have you."

Adolphe walked Père Gilles to the door as Placide stood watching the two men. "Thank you for coming at such an early hour," Adolphe said.

"It was a blessing. Please consider it, I would love for you both to attend as well. It would be the perfect service."

Placide's head jerked towards the door. "Pardon me?"

"We would love to, Mon Père. I'll be in touch," Adolphe said as he closed the door.

Adolphe returned to Placide. In response to his friend's

exasperated, accusatory speechlessness, Adolphe responded, "Dust off your good suit, dear Placide."

Boston 2005

F ive days before the show, Bryn distributed the new charts to the musicians. Each player seemed to have the same look of confusion as they took the new pages. Had they missed something? Was this some kind of joke? They eventually saw that it was not, but a new reality. Among their quizzical glances, Bryn's fragile hope remained intact.

"I'm sure you're all wondering what this is. I've been struggling with the arrangement for some time, not satisfied with how it represented this sacred song. I finally told someone and they encouraged me to do something about it. I hadn't respected the original work as I should and I think that showed. I hope you can understand."

There was silence for a brief moment as the musicians processed what Bryn had told them, but acceptance quickly followed. The first violinist spoke to Bryn as if on behalf of the group, "You got it, maestro." Countless others nodded their agreement.

Bryn returned a thankful acknowledgment. "Alright then, take a few moments to look it over and make your own markings, then we'll come back together in five."

As the musicians began their review, the rear auditorium

doors opened. Hall and Charles walked in together towards the stage. Bryn stepped from the platform to meet them halfway. He had considered many of the implications for his massive change to the arrangement, but it only now dawned on him that Hall too would need to know about them. The key, tempo, and all the cues had changed.

Bryn met Hall in the center aisle, fresh score in hand. "I wanted to give you this." He felt no need to explain his reasons to Hall; he wouldn't understand them. "We made some changes to the arrangement."

Hall blinked, surprised. Bryn saw something in his expression he had not anticipated: excitement. That's when it dawned on him that Hall thought the changes were what he had suggested. "Smart man, I knew you would see it eventually."

Before Bryn was able to correct him, Hall brushed past him, ascending the stairs to the stage. Bryn looked to Charles, who simply shrugged with a smirk. Both men knew the implications of letting Hall think the changes were his ideas, but Bryn decided to let it play out. He returned to the platform, clapping twice to gain the attention of the musicians.

"Let's start from the beginning." He raised his hands, simultaneously waving and counting the measures leading in. When the first beat of the piece came, the cellos entered softly. The others remained attentive, gaze in-tune with both Bryn and their own sheet. Each could instantly sense the incoming verse, so much so that some eyes even bounced to Hall in expectation. When the entrance came, Bryn cued both the breath and the first words, but Hall did not enter, nor did he realize he had missed the cue.

Bryn swiped his hands across his body to stop the music. He turned to Hall, "My fault, I didn't cue you well. Let's take it again, and I'll come in with you this time."

Flushed with embarrassment, Hall nodded his understanding. Again, Bryn raised his hands, waving and counting the leading measure before cuing the cellos. The few measures before Hall's entrance were gruesomely slow, Bryn's stomach tying itself into concerned knots. When the moment arrived, Bryn made sure that he gave Hall an exaggerated cue, softly singing the entrance along with him.

Thankfully, Hall entered on time and kept the pace. Though he began flat, he quickly was able to find the appropriate notes with some help from Bryn. But no one felt at ease, all concerned by the uncertainty with which Hall carried his part. Bryn was thankful for the talent of the musicians, because they were driving themselves as he devoted his entire effort to keeping Hall on-track.

It was not until the key change that Bryn could see the problem, which was much too late. He noticed Hall's higher register becoming more strained, chin stretching upward, struggling to grab hold of the next note. He was also sure that others noticed too, because eyes drifted worriedly to the vocalist. Bryn instantly thought forward, knowing that Hall was going to lose runway before reaching the climax of the bridge. Everyone present knew that fact, except for Hall himself. Because surely if he had known the train was going to crash, he would have stopped before it did.

As with all disasters, nobody moved a muscle when if first arrived. Hall's chin was pointed upward, face reddened from the effort that caused his neck to strain. His voice sounded as if it was strangling itself, because after a single breath's sound passed over the vocal folds, the sound was cut short by an inability to sustain. Hall stopped, shocked by his own failure.

Bryn swiped his hands to stop the orchestra, but there was no need; the orchestra had stopped on their own.

Bryn nervously looked to Hall, guilty he had allowed him to get to that point. But he also was unsure how to fix it. He couldn't change the key, because he had specifically placed it back in the original. Plus, he would have to transpose and reprint for everyone. But he also knew that there was no world in which Hall would be able to hit that note. Especially in the next five days. And Hall knew it too.

Hall threw his score at Bryn, hitting him in the side. "Why'd you make these changes? It was good before, I want to go back to that." His cheeks had not lost their embarrassed flush. He spoke loudly, but his voice bore no confidence.

Bryn was amused by this sudden turn of opinion, remembering the last rehearsal when he made it clear he wanted some major changes. Reliving that moment in his mind, Bryn knew that there was no place for Hall in this piece. That's when he stopped trying to preserve any.

"This is the arrangement now." He did not yell or use hostile inflection, plainly stating the matter-of-fact decision. Hall desperately examined Bryn's expression for any ounce of second guessing, any sliver of doubt that could provide hope for him to get his way. He found none. He quickly rushed off the stage, walking briskly down the aisle, stopping near Charles.

"This is the arrangement now," Charles said, more sternly than Bryn. With one futile glance back to the orchestra, Hall could see each and every face gazing back on him with an expression he hadn't seen in ages: pity. He turned without a word, fleeing the auditorium one last time.

Neither Bryn, nor Charles, nor the majority of the musicians felt a twinge of sadness over the loss of Hall. Instead, they felt free from the nuisance of Hall. Bryn had no issue regaining control, everyone was looking to him for guidance once Hall had departed. He allowed a smile to find his face, briefly glancing at Charles as it did so. "Let's keep it going. I guess we can run the piece a few times without vocals. I'll step in for the feature's part once just so we can get a feel for it."

For the rest of rehearsal, everyone was in sync. Each musician played with skill and poise, confirming their placement in the esteemed group. By the third run, their joy and passion for the art was obvious, infectious even. On the fifth run, Bryn stepped to the side of the orchestra. He counted the orchestra in, before ceasing his conducting, allowing them to continue on their own. Then, when the time came, he sang.

His voice carried without restraint, elegantly floating across the auditorium like snow carried on the winter breeze. His flourishes were swirls of wind, tossing and turning but never detracting from the forward-moving beauty. He felt calm, more settled in this role that reminded him of his musical roots. But most impressively, his execution of the high note in the bridge was effortless, which did not go unnoticed.

After the rehearsal had wrapped and the musicians departed, Charles and Bryn remained in the performance hall. "We should probably talk about today," Charles eventually said.

Bryn nodded. "I know, I'm not sure where we go from here. I'm glad he's gone, but we still need a vocalist."

Charles laughed, "I didn't mean that, there are tons of people who can sing. I wanted to talk about the arrangement. I hadn't heard it yet."

Bryn looked at him curiously. "What'd you think?"

"I think it's your best work. It made me see what you were saying about the other one. This one carries the respect and reverence the song deserves. Well done, maestro." He turned to leave, but stopped himself with a final thought. "It was good to see you like that again today, when you were singing. Reminds me of when we were in Chamber Singers."

"Like what?"

With a wry smile that showed his gratitude, Charles responded, "Joyful."

Brant Rock 1906

The sound of Reginald Fessenden's foot anxiously tapping the floor bled from his office, through the hallways as he scanned the contents of his memo box. He shuffled the sheets to peruse the headers of the pages, internal memos and crumpled letters addressed to his office. Each telegram and transcript conveyed a different variation of the same urgency: in the prospects of innovation, someone must act. Reginald's glance slowed as he came across the summarizing incident report regarding the failure of the broadcasting tower mere weeks ago, taking the time to scan it. "…[the] structure collapsed due to inadequate and improper construction. The question should not be why did this fail, but why not sooner…" read the external assessment. He tossed it on his desk, adding to the heap.

With no greeting, the door to Reginald's office opened swiftly, forcing his attention from the pages. It was his associate, Stein. "Mr. Fessenden, Mr. Reed and Mr. Pickerd have arrived. Should I lead them to the testing area?"

Reginald took a moment, searching his memories for the men as he remembered they had written requesting to attend the test. "Thank you Stein, that will work nicely. Please let them know I'll join them shortly." As Stein turned to exit, Reginald caught his attention once more. "You've seen most of these," he gestured to the memos, "anything I need to know for today?"

Stein looked upward absently, thinking. "Dr. Kennedy and some others expressed their apologies for not being able to attend today's demonstration. Professor Trowbridge couldn't make it because his wife is ill."

Reginald nodded his head in acknowledgment. "Of course, we'll be sure to have some flowers sent. Thanks."

"Yes, sir," Stein said leaving the room. Reginald attempted to straighten the pages without success, instead shaking them from his thoughts as he picked up his coat and checked his watch again. The time for the demonstration was quickly approaching and he knew he shouldn't be late. He began walking towards the labs where he asked Stein to take the visitors.

Arriving at the door of the room, he took one deep concentrating breath, and confidently made his entrance. "Hello gentleman, I hope you haven't been waiting too long." Upon scanning the faces of the three men, Reginald could see the unspoken relief in Stein's face as his conversational rescue had arrived. It would seem that Pickerd and Reed had been less than enthused to be there, so Reginald altered his tone. "What's wrong? Are you eager to witness some history?"

Mr. Pickerd spoke reservedly, with none of Reginald's excitement. "That would be nice. Unfortunately, I'm more concerned with witnessing a few thousand dollars being wasted; yet again."

"Now Mr. Pickerd, you know great things aren't achieved without some risk," Reginald said playfully.

As Reginald spoke, Professor Thompson walked in, catching the end of the conversation. "Fessenden, his concerns are valid. We can't pretend that the tower didn't collapse last week. I know that a lot of our funds from GE were tied up in that endeavor, and we can't sacrifice the financial position of our own organizations if we're not seeing positive results." Reginald quickly shook the surprise from his face. Thompson had always been direct and honest, but Reginald hadn't expected him to be so candid about his financial positions. Not this soon, anyway.

"Agreed, we feel the same way," Mr. Reed added.

Reginald attempted to slip some understanding into his response. "I see. You can only invest in theory for so long, and I'm extremely grateful for your support. That's why today is exciting, because we're finally moving these concepts in a practical and applicable direction. I know I'm excited."

Reginald excused himself to make final adjustments to the hardware. As he did so, a handful of other observers and staff members trickled in to observe the demonstration. He'd extended an invitation to a few departments and was touched to see their support. Once he felt prepared, he returned to the small crowd that had gathered. "I want to thank everyone for being here. Let's get this test moving, shall we? Mr. Stein?" At his mention, Stein uncovered the three microphones that had been positioned on a table near the front of the room. They were surrounded by various wired and rotating wheels, all intertwined to comprise one machine.

"If I may, could I have two volunteers to accompany Mr. Stein to our receiving station in Plymouth? It's a few miles, but perfect for our test today." Reginald asked. The attendees tentatively looked back and forth at one another. Eventually, Mr. Pickerd and a gentleman from the Associated Press accepted. "Perfect, please follow Mr. Stein."

As the three men exited, Reginald addressed the remaining visitors. "We'll give them time to travel, so feel free to look around and examine everything." The crowd murmured and dispersed, visiting with one another. Reginald noticed Mr. Thompson's interest in the device, migrating towards him.

"So what have we here? Some type of alternator?" Thompson asked.

Reginald nodded with a smile. "It is, good eye. This is our modified high-frequency alternator. It runs about 50 kHz on a continuous RF wavelength." He noticed Thompson's interest in the hardware. "We're fortunate in that we were given one of only a few of these in existence. The designer really wants to help us succeed." Reginald eyed Mr. Thompson as he halfheartedly examined the machinery. He looked as if he was trying to busy himself, dancing around an uncomfortable thought.

"Reginald, I didn't want to tell you today but you need to hear it. Our Board is trying to move funding elsewhere. They've told me that if there's not evident progress, we've got to drop our contributions for the next year."

Reginald blinked for a few seconds. Deftly, he responded, "I understand. Let's hope that doesn't have to happen." He took a deep breath, more appreciative of Thompson's honesty than concerned by the news. "I almost forgot. These microphones are special too. They're carbon microphones. I've made some small alterations to the two on the right while leaving the third unchanged. Plus the newly constructed antennas we fitted this system with. There's quite a bit to go right today."

Mr. Thompson gave a sympathetic, sorrowful half smile. He patted Reginald's shoulder. "I believe in you. Now give me something we can show them."

Reginald looked at the clock on the wall, judging it had been long enough for the small group to make it to Plymouth.

He spoke loudly for everyone to hear, "Gentlemen, if you will gather round the table, we can begin the demonstration." He slipped between the group and engaged the alternator's motor. Before doing so, he addressed the room once more. "Please refrain from talking among yourselves while we are transmitting. It makes reception a little difficult if there is extra noise added."

His heart began to steadily increase the speed and intensity of its work, causing his breath to nervously increase too. They had done their own tests privately, but something about an audience always toyed with his confidence. He said a silent prayer as he stepped to flip the switch. He engaged the alternator, which began slowly and sped to a loud, continuous rumble. Once it reached its stable revolutions, Reginald stepped to the leftmost microphone. Before speaking, he addressed the group in the room. "Here goes nothing!" Leaning forward, he pressed the button to open his channel. He spoke with power and intentional diction, his lips almost brushing the microphone's head. "Testing. Testing. This is Reginald Fessenden transmitting from the Brant Rock testing facility."

Reginald released the button as he turned to address the group over his shoulder. "Who's next? Mr. Davis, how about giving it a whirl?" Mr. Davis looked back in surprise, but stepped forward to oblige. Reginald patted the chair next to his, positioned in front of the middle microphone in which Davis positioned himself. "When you're ready, hold this button down and speak clearly. When you're done."

Mr. Davis sat straighter in the chair, finding the right tone. He then leaned over the microphone, pressing the button. "Hello everyone, this is Davis. Hope you can hear me loud and clear." His volume increased throughout the statement, so much so that he nearly shouted the final words.

Fessenden clapped in approval. He again turned his head towards the group to select someone for the final microphone. He pointed to a man near the door. "You're here with the Associated Press, right? Why don't you send a message to your colleague?"

The man's eyes widened nervously as he stood frozen. Eventually, someone beside him gently nudged him along towards the microphones, where Davis pulled out the chair and gave him a reassuring glance. The man sat, leaning forward and pressing the button. His speech was much quieter than the others, making it almost impossible for anyone to distinguish what he had said into the microphone. Before anyone could ask him to clarify, he had risen to return to the crowd.

Reginald leaned forward again, speaking clearly into the microphone. "Mr. Stein, kindly send us a telegram if you are receiving us. If not, this has been a bit embarrassing. Powering off now." He quickly stood, cutting the machine in order to hear better, and moved quickly to the wire across the room. The room had followed him to the wire, a collective breath held in anticipation. Almost immediately, the short, pulsating clicks tapped clearly: Y-E-S.

The crew began cheering, clapping and congratulating one another on the success of the test. As the shouts continued, Reginald caught the eye of Mr. Thompson from the other side of the room, whose smile was wider than any other.

…

Mr. Stein returned to Brant Rock shortly along with the others. They described the clarity of the voices transmitted. As they spoke, Mr. Davis led Reginald to the corner of the room to address him more privately. "Reginald, I've never experienced anything like this. It will change how we communicate forever, and I thank you for letting me witness it. If you have the time, I would like to discuss it further in detail." He waved his notebook. "Possibly for the record? I think this will be a featured piece if you'd allow it. Just want to be sure I'm presenting everything correctly." Reginald agreed, fielding multiple reporter's requests before they each boarded the departing train the following afternoon.

Roquemaure 1847

dolphe's tap of the baton echoed against the marble walls of the sanctuary as he held his hand skyward to collect everyone's attention. "Let's take that pickup into the chorus again, this time with more alto. Emily, ready?" He asked, glancing at the featured vocalist who serenely nodded acknowledgment. His eyes found the choir once more. He raised his baton, suspended in the air. "Perfect, let's begin. Two, three, four..."

Every voice began at once, the words *Fall on your knees* crashing into the halls around them. As their voices billowed like a wave in the turbulent night, Placide's head couldn't help but drift upward distractedly. He glanced again at the panels of stained glass, for the hundredth time in rehearsal, unable to look away from the small lamb that lay in a pasture with a crown of greenery on its head, eyes solemnly staring back into his own.

Placide clenched his eyes tightly, but still saw the phantom of the lamb even when he did so. He focused on the music, letting the crash of the sound waves slam and throw him, helpless against the tide of his own thoughts. But the more he allowed in, the more he found himself struck by feelings of unworthiness that had been slipping into his thoughts ever since Adolphe shared the piece. Had he done wrong? He had written verses about humility and submission, but the boldness and indictment that once fueled him had changed. Did the words still feel right?

Placide spent enough time in his own thoughts that he barely noticed Adolphe clapping. "Wonderful job everyone. Truly spectacular. This is a special project. I'm thankful you are lending your voices to it. Let's end there for today." Adolphe bid each musician farewell as they slowly left the sanctuary, smiling. Once the final musician had gone, Adolphe descended the stairs and found Placide in one of the rearmost pews. He sat beside him, both men keeping their eyes sternly forward, affixed to the stained glass.

Placide first spoke. "I'm not sure I recognize it anymore. That's probably a good thing, since I was harsh in my words." He paused, waiting for Adolphe to speak. When he did not, Placide continued, "I think it scares me, the way you were able to polish my words into something... like this. It's like pieces of my heart, pieces I hadn't even known about, are going to be on display for everyone to see. I don't trust it debuting here."

Adolphe sighed. "If you want healing or reconciliation, there's going to have to be some grace. Grace to this church, these people, Père Gilles, but also yourself. You believe these words, words that came from you, yet also demand their own importance to be shared far and wide. I think you deserve for people to hear them, and I think these people deserve to hear them."

Placide slumped slightly, his exhaustion ever evident. The mental weight of the last few days had not been obvious to Adolphe. "I don't know what I believe anymore, Adolphe. I feel like the only thing remotely certain is that I don't want to be here. I don't belong here."

"I wish you wouldn't give up so easily."

"I do not belong here, Adolphe," Placide said again sharply, his voice echoing its power. Both sat silently, surprised by the intensity. Placide brushed imaginary dust off his trousers as he attempted to shift his tone. "It is beautiful, and I believe you are responsible for the majority of it. It's your best work, regardless of how I feel about it."

Adolphe nodded curtly. "Thank you. So is that all you wanted to say?"

Placide surprised them both with what he said next. "I'm going to attend the mass." Adolphe turned to face him finally as Placide quickly set the record straight. "But I'm sitting in the back, only here as support. I don't want to be recognized or, really, seen at all. I just want to be here to support you and to hear the final product."

Adolphe muttered his agreement as Placide moved, sliding from the pew. "If I don't see you before then, good luck dear friend." He quietly exited the sanctuary.

When his friend had left and his thoughts slowed, Adolphe did what he had done each night since the inception of the song. He slid from the pew onto his knees, bowing his head in prayer. He lifted a prayer of thanksgiving for the words and the music, for the performers and for his friend. For Père Gilles and this church. Most of all, he prayed the song would be the vessel for so many ears that needed to hear. And he prayed his gratitude for the salvation that was offered to those that sought it.

Tennessee 2015

Lucy turned the porch light on as she and Annie let themselves in the door. Their grocery bags were filled to the brim, making entering her parent's house a two-woman effort. As Annie removed the key from the lock, holding the door with her heel for her mother, she called out, "Grandma, we're here." They entered, setting the bags on the counter.

"Merry Christmas, girls," said Grandma, shuffling slowly into the kitchen. She wrapped her arms around Annie, then moved to do the same to Lucy. With her arm still on Lucy's shoulder, Grandma examined the bags. "What's this?"

Annie and Lucy looked at one another before Lucy answered, winking. "I told you, we've got dinner covered."

"I'd assumed you would pick up a pizza or bring some leftovers." Grandma's eyes showed her excitement. "This is a nice surprise."

"We thought something fresh would be nice. Soup and cornbread, hope you like it," Annie said. All three laughed, because it was a staple of Grandma's.

"How's dad?" Lucy asked, changing the tone.

Grandma sighed, shaking her head, disappointed by the news she was delivering. "It's hard to tell these days. Now that he can't talk to us, I just have to guess if it's a good day or not. But I can see in his eyes that he's drifting." She paused, letting the silence soften the blow of what she really thought. "We're probably nearing the end." Lucy and Annie could see the weariness in her eyes, the combination of age and sadness carving deep lines that riddled her face.

"I'm gonna go say hello," Annie said as she unpacked the last bag, gently touching Grandma's arm as she walked past.

Grandma rolled up her sleeves, moving to the sink. "Alright, I can cut the vegetables."

"Mom, I can do this. Why don't you take a seat and relax. I know you're tired."

Grandma slowly turned the water off, not allowing herself to look at her daughter for fear of letting her see the pleading in her expression. "Please, let me help. I feel like all I do these days is sit by and watch. I just want to feel useful."

Her words cut Lucy unexpectedly. She picked up the vegetables and placed them on the counter next to her mother. Without responding, she gave her a short embrace before locating the pot she needed.

...

You lay, your eyes closed in the medical bed, mind drifting between lucidity and the void between.

Days, weeks, seconds between your words with M–,
her angelic soothing voice tuned
to the heartstrings of your soul.
Floating to sea, the beams guiding you
through the rocks that strike your hull.

How long since I fed myself?
  your sorry soul asks the stranger.
  He can't even see your pain
  his eyes following the world around him
  ceaselessly searching your answers.

How long 'til the rock's cleft
  when a body can be loosed the body's curse?
  Seventh day seeking still
  when the clay has dried from
  the wind blown through it.

A– does she see you?
  A– does she hear you?
  The flame carried from the
  torch you once lit.
  Exult, dreamer, your sleep can wait.

...

Annie entered the living room to greet her grandfather. The room had drastically changed over the last few months. A large medical bed now rested in the center of the room that once held space for many others. All the seating had been removed and replaced with two chairs from the kitchen table for visitors. There was a small table positioned within eyesight of the bed which had pictures and cards propped up for Grandpa to see.

She was happy to notice that, despite the changes in the room, the large record cabinet was still in its same spot. It was probably too heavy to move, but she was glad it stayed nonetheless. She pulled a seat next to the bed, taking his heavy hand in her own. His skin was tough and worn, her thumb rubbing mindlessly over its creases. "Merry Christmas, Grandpa." She raised the hand tenderly to her lips. She masked the pain she felt as his glazed eyes barely noticed her presence. "Mom's here too, she's in the kitchen. We're cooking tonight." She motioned towards the table. "That's a lot of cards. Looks like you're a popular guy." As the silence grew, she was reminded how difficult it was to speak to someone when they couldn't speak to you. Still, she continued on for him.

"Dad stopped by Uncle Joseph's to help hang a light. They'll all be over later. Aunt Ginny and the kids too." Her eyes panned around the room, noticing the indentations in the carpet where the furniture used to be. That's what this room reminded her of: a life, a room, a relationship that once was, ever altered by the horrid visage of time. But pressed on the other side of that coin was the realization of the now. The essence of such realities came to a stop when her eyes found the record cabinet.

Annie smiled, "How about some music?" She stood to make a selection, her eyes passed over album after album that filled her with memories. Every summer, she would spend a day or two each week in this house. The mornings were for exploring the yard, playing with the inventions of her own imagination. After lunch, the afternoon sun proving too hot to tolerate, she would select an album with Grandpa. In this living room, they would lie on their backs on the floor as they listened to her selection. They were quiet, save for Grandpa's occasional hums of melody or laughs when his favorite chords hit.

Her eyes moved to the beginning of the row, remembering that Grandpa kept Christmas records there, outside of his regular alphabetization for easy selection. It didn't take her long to find it; her heart already guiding before she had realized its directions. Her finger slid against the spine, gently retrieving it from the shelf. *The Christmas Song* read the cover. Removing the disc gently from the sleeve, giving the flat surface a blow for good measure, she laid it on the turntable and switched the system on, along with the speakers. As the disc turned, she lowered the needle carefully.

Everyone was familiar with that opening track by Nat King Cole; it had practically ruled the airwaves in coffee shops and stores for the better part of a month already. But something about hearing the pop of the needle's first contact followed by the two piano chords and soaring strings billow from these distinct units made the song feel completely different. She stood back, hands on her hips as she listened to those first lines about the open fire. She turned, "I better help mom in the kitchen. I'll come back to flip it over."

...

Something in those opening strings brings you back, remembering.

What sweet melodies of past
  summer afternoons, you lay on the carpet
  while a hum leaves your lungs.
  You know this one, right?
  You know it's essence to its presence

A– picked it out, the sounds her choice.
  Taking the sleeve from the shelf
  filled with years gone by
  she starts your journey,
  your journey of lucidity.

Where is the path
   to spring's warming light
   shining through the bough of
   the royal magnolia blossoms.
   They tumble in the yearning wind.

Your hour has neared, but you must still say goodbye…

…

Grandma angled her head slightly to hear the song spilling from the living room. She gave Annie a smile as she walked by. "I'm glad you put that one on, he'll love it. Those records haven't been played in a while."

Lucy cocked her ear too, smiling. "I can't make it out, what'd you pick?"

"Nat King Cole," Annie said, washing her hands.

Lucy's smile broadened with recognition. "His favorite."

Annie began to gather the ingredients for the cornbread. As she was opening the package of cornmeal, Grandma asked, "Did you two make it to the recital? Joseph showed me the videos, they both did so good. I wish I had been there."

"Yeah, they both did a great job. It was a packed crowd," Annie said as she emptied scoops into a mixing bowl.

Lucy paused her measuring. "Did Joey play the video for dad? I bet he would have loved hearing it."

"He did, and I'm sure he loved it," Grandma said quietly.

In the lull that followed, Annie heard the chorus of *I Saw Three Ships* as she finished mixing the wet and dry ingredients. She wiped her hands absently on her thighs, walking back to the living room anticipating the need to flip the disc after *O*

Holy Night.

...

You see the clouds move on,
 the coming serenity heralded
 by the brightness and vision.
 Your eyes subtly moving for the
 first time of your own volition.

As they drift to the corner
 walls gone and space wide open
 you see the irises of your Father
 long ago moved beyond but
 the glacial blue seen in L–.

Carry my soul, you say
 to the outstretched hands that
 move to lift you from your
 fallen grace. Your face turns back
 to see where you once were.

Your thankfulness is coupled with
 the thoughts of your own
 children you leave in the past.
 To see your girls once more
 to take your eyes from the eyes that see you.

Give them a sign, you'd say
 as your soul and flesh
 pull at the seam of their binding.

As you have been delivered,
   you ask that they too find it.

The hand of your past lifts as
   the breath moves from your lungs
   to hum once more.
   Make sweet music, you command,
   as you serve as an instrument once more.

...

Grandma glanced around when she noticed Annie hadn't begun preheating the oven. She wiped her hands as she walked into the living room to ask if she should pour the batter. Soon, Lucy noticed the absence of her kitchen mates. She didn't have time to wonder where they had gone. From the living room she heard the low, crackling hum of someone following the record's melody.

Lucy sprinted through the kitchen, down the hall to the living room where the sound was coming from. When she reached the doorway, she saw that her mother and Annie were holding one another in a soft embrace, sniffing the tears away. They stood looking at her father in the bed. As her eyes moved to him, seeing that his eyes were closed and his hand raised in front of him, waving unsteadily in time with the lyrics of *O Holy Night*. The hum had been his.

As she stepped into the embrace with her mother and daughter, three generations holding each other closely, she felt her own eyes well with tears. In the glory of the final chorus, she whispered aloud, "Thank you, Lord, for giving him one more song to sing."

Movement IV: Finale

Fort Campbell 2004

Chaplain Andrews,

It was good to finally hear from you. I must admit, I was beginning to wonder if I was going to receive your report. I have seen many prepare intensely only to be scared away from the calling once they face the true job: ministering to those on the brink of hopelessness in the midst of war.

I've had your last letter on my mind constantly. The Lord works in the most interesting, unexpected ways. The simplicity of one song to bring both you and Daniels closer to Him at the same time shows how in even the most critical moments of our faith, He can refocus us with one small gesture. He reminds us of His love every day.

Your letter also stirred a memory from my early days in ministry, when I had just arrived in the Philippines. Much like now, Christmas was just around the corner and I found myself trying to reach troops who had lost their hope. Of course, my own hope felt distant. I had grown close to some of the other men of faith stationed with me. Despite our differences in beliefs, we could each relate to the struggles of ministering in a war zone.

I found myself particularly drawn to Chaplain Adler, who was a minister of the Jewish faith. I found his company to be level-headed, despite our major discrepancies in belief. Honestly, I think it was refreshing for us both to have kind, thoughtful conversations with one another because it subverted what we had been conditioned to expect.

On Christmas Eve, after a meal in the dining hall, I led a small service for those who wished to attend. It was conveniently a Sunday, so most were free from duties to stop in. To my surprise, Chaplain Adler attended the service. He stood in the back, only reading the liturgies from certain sections, but he was attentive. His presence meant a great deal to me.

After the service, I made a point to express my appreciation. When I approached him, I noticed a folded booklet in his hand. We exchanged greetings and he handed me the booklet. He told me it was a small Hanukkah gift, though some would frown on his having given it to me. I cherished the gesture, before I even knew what it contained. He said someone had passed it along to him, thinking he would appreciate the Hebrew story, but he had a feeling I would find it more impactful. When I'd returned to my quarters and read it, I found the following story:

Yusif struck the door powerfully with his open palm, rattling its hinges. The house belonged to a distant relative that he'd not seen for years but was certain would have room for them; he had sent word weeks before. Of course, these were rational thoughts that comforted him before arriving here. Now, his wife screamed in agony with each passing contraction as she clung to the donkey that carried her.

"Avnar, please open the door. I'm begging you," Yusif yelled breathlessly.

Avnar opened the door slightly, restricting it from opening fully with his body. "Yusif, what are you doing here?"

"Avnar, my apologies, but we need room here with you. And we need help immediately. She's in labor as we speak."

Avnar stood unmoving. "Yusif, there is no space here. All of our family is in town for the census, you understand." He tried to close the door but Yusif stopped him.

"Please, I sent word to Talya weeks ago. She assured me that we could stay here."

Avnar tried to remain polite. "I'm sorry if she misinformed you, but we are full. You cannot stay here."

Yusif's wife Miriam let out a loud, strained cry of pain. The sound caused both men to turn their heads, concern washing over Yusif's face again.

"Please Avnar, we only need a few hours. This child cannot be born in the street. We need help."

Avnar stepped outside, closing the door behind him. Certain no others could hear him, he dropped the guise of politeness. "I don't think that would be a good idea. Given what is about to happen, I wouldn't want to inconvenience anyone with purification rites."

"We can stay away from everyone." Yusif said.

"Yusif, enough. Must I say it outright? Everyone knows the sin which dishonored this conception. I'm shocked to hear you say wife, for we know the union has not been consummated. I will not have an adulteress birthing under my roof. Leave, please."

Yusif was in disbelief. In his frustration, he walked away without responding. He took the reins of the donkey, leading them further along the road. As he continued to pound doors, helplessly begging for kindness, he found none. People feared his desperation, feared his pleas. They feared the prospect of new life taking breath under their roof.

However, a stranger overheard Yusif's requests from afar and walked slowly to meet him between houses. "If you need help, follow *me." Weighed from the constant rejection, Yusif did not immediately respond. The man continued, more earnest than before. "Listen, I don't have much, but I do have a roof that is yours. Better than the road. I heard you needed help. I want to help."*

Yusif considered his words, finding them reassuring. A spirit deep within him encouraged him, so he moved. "Can you send for some help?"

"Don't worry, my wife is home, and she has helped bring many children into this world."

They soon arrived at a small shack surrounded with livestock, the sheep and goats roaming the land on either side. "I know it's small, but the lower floor is open. The animals have been out roaming all day and can stay out as long as you need."

Yusif tied the donkey and assisted Miriam as she dismounted, slowly, with difficulty. As Yusif led her inside, the homeowner went to tell his wife about the visitors. To everyone's surprise, she entered the room quickly, as if she had already been informed of the news. She was confident, making Miriam comfortable and sending the men to retrieve supplies. They retrieved blankets and sackcloth, the husband clearing out a manger for the baby to be laid in if need be. He filled it with straw and fabric scraps in an effort to make it softer and warmer.

Miriam did not labor long, her time being near. She began to push before Yusif and the husband had stepped out. When they had realized the closeness, the husband stepped outside as Yusif stood frozen. In a fog of existential separation between what he saw and understood, Yusif was a bystander as his wife courageously continued to push, each accompanied by a guttural outcry.

With the loudest scream yet, the woman caught something with the cloth she had been positioning between Miriam's legs, her arms moving fast. Wiping the small form, she allowed herself a relieved smile. For a brief moment, everyone held a collective breath as they craned to look at the new person. After what seemed like an eternity, the child cried. "Praise be to Adonai," the woman exclaimed.

In that moment, Yusif walked to Miriam, who held the child, and his confusion disappeared, purpose and meaning extinguishing any concern. As he crouched, wrapping his arms around her, she whispered in his ear, "Praise be to Adonai."

"Praise be to Adonai," he echoed.

"Mazel tov. Have you considered a name?" asked the woman.

Yusif nodded, turning to Miriam for her to answer. She could feel the tightening of her throat, fresh tears constricting her words. Fresh tears still continued to trickle as love filled the name she spoke. "His name shall be Yeshua."

The story was torn there, ending the narrative. I'm sure there was something about the angels singing or wise men following the star, but we all know that story. Instead the text left me with the story of a man and woman experiencing the very natural panic of the imminent birth of their son. It reminded me of the humanity of Christ; humanity that further shows his magnificence. He came to earth as flesh and still lived the perfect life, later to be killed for us that couldn't do the same.

I was struck by the story, but also by Adler's gesture. I intended to repay the kindness. I attended his service that evening, the fifth day of Hanukkah being observed. He made a point to mention that with this day, the number of lit candles of the menorah exceeds the number of those not lit, emphasizing the importance of being the light in dark places. It was wonderful to realize he was practicing the very message he preached by giving me that gift.

Though our faiths are substantially different, Adler and I

have maintained a friendship that has been a source of great comfort to me. When he retired a few years ago, I was saddened to see him go, but proud of the time we spent in each other's company. I still keep that booklet folded in my breast pocket, occasionally taking it out to read every now and again. I've almost memorized it by now, but holding the gift from my friend makes it all the more special.

I hope you cherish the gift you were given when you experienced that song with Daniels. From your report, I'm certain he'll remember the gift it was to him. What I hope most is that one day you can share it with another Chaplain down the line. Our calling is noble but strenuous, and few choose the strenuous life. But there are obviously gifts that make it worthwhile.

Peace and blessings to you this Christmas. I'm grateful for your call of duty and for the impact you've had on Daniels.

Praying ceaselessly for you,

Chaplain Michaels

Brant Rock 1906

Reginald Fessenden leaned against the bridge's railing as he watched the ships pass. He'd been itching for something to do, his thoughts not slowing to match the pace of the holidays. He'd given the staff an extended vacation for Christmas which had been welcomed after the emotional stress of the collapsing tower and success of the radio transmissions. But now, on Christmas Eve, he wandered the silent grounds of the Brant Rock facility, searching for solace.

The brisk wind from the sea saturated the air with salt. Fessenden kept warm with the chipped glass he refilled with scotch. The bottle had been a gift from Mr. Thompson after the success of the transmissions the prior week, but Fessenden had waited to open it until he felt more like savoring it. It sat in his office, the bottle shuffled around as the final workweek of the year concluded.

As he sipped, the dark liquid burning him from the inside out, he thought of the successful test. He thought of his lifelong dream, to bring easy, clear, timely communication to the masses. This had been a significant step toward that. He imagined a future where people's voices could be transmitted from house to house; information and entertainment passing through the airwaves. He imagined how these broadcasts could bring the world together.

Reginald heard the soft click of footsteps on the wooden deck, the sound steadily increasing as someone approached. "Hi sweetie, ready to go inside?" asked his wife as she hugged him tightly.

He pulled her gently to him. "Let's stay here a moment." She brushed the railing before leaning against it too. They looked over the water for a moment, allowing the sound of the waves and rushing air to occupy all sonic space.

She took his hand in hers, "I'm proud of you, Reg. This has been your dream and it's finally coming true." He smiled at her, grateful. She paused, looking out at the sea once more. There were two ships passing in the distance. "It's a shame that they have to be out there at Christmas time. I'm thankful for their work, but everyone deserves to celebrate Christmas with their loved ones."

Reginald stood away from the railing, turning to look at his wife. "Do we have a little more time? I think I just had an idea."

"Sure, what is it?"

He grinned, taking her hand once more. "I think we can spread a little Christmas cheer."

• • •

"Could you hand me that microphone on the left?" he asked his wife. They had entered the facility and collected a few items from Reginald's office before setting up in the testing room. Reginald had pushed his phonograph down the hall, wedging it through the doorway as his wife followed carrying his bible and violin.

"Tell me again who is going to hear this?" asked Mrs. Fessenden.

"I can't say for certain, but potentially anyone in, say, a hundred miles who hears the alert and tunes in. I'm not sure of the actual range on this transmitter yet, we haven't gotten the information on that." Reginald finished setting up the phonograph before ensuring all the wires were correctly plugged. "Alright, I think we're good to go. I'm going to start the alternator, then send out the alert. I guess we'll go from there." As he turned, Reginald's wife held his arm for a moment, before tenderly kissing his cheek.

Fessenden started the alternator and walked to the transmitter, hoping it got someone's attention. He clicked the characters "-.-. −.-/ -.-. −.-/ -.-. −.-" (CQ, CQ, CQ) to alert the airwaves of a special message. Breathing deeply, he walked the three steps to the microphone and took a seat. "Good evening and Happy Christmas. This is Reginald Fessenden broadcasting from the Brant Rock testing facility. We have been working on some revolutionary methods of communication and wanted to use them to spread cheer on the eve of our Savior's birth. Though we are far and wide, some separated from our loved ones, I hope these next few moments bring you peace and joy this season. First, here is a recorded piece by the great Handel."

Fessenden moved the microphone to rest inches from the phonograph. He gave the crank a few rotations before moving and dropping the needle to play the piece, sitting back to listen intently. He heard the cracks and static over the sounds of the running alternator and smiled, because others would be hearing it too. In fact, this might be one of the first musical broadcasts in the history of radio reception.

As the song neared its conclusion, Fessenden retrieved his violin and returned to the microphone. He waited for Handel's piece to finish before beginning the next. As he raised his bow, he quietly slipped into the melody of his favorite song, the song his mother taught him as a young boy, *O Holy Night*.

It was one of the first tunes he learned on the violin, its notes second nature to his fingers. After the first chorus, he felt himself approaching the bridge, humming as the natural crescendo enticed him to do so. When he had closed his eyes in deep connection to the music, his hum shifted to the words of the chorus. He saw images of himself as a boy, attending midnight mass as they sang the very same words. He sang them in unison with his family then, his parents and siblings holding hands.

He recalled his parents taking the Eucharist, their prayers lingering as the cup found their lips. He remembered the words of the Psalms of David, the prophecies of Ezekiel being part of the liturgies. Finally, as he sang the final words of the chorus, he returned to the moment he was living at Brant Rock. He gently placed the violin and bow on the table and lifted the bible that sat before him.

Roquemaure 1847

Placide did not enter the church until he heard both the organ and congregation's music. Hoping to avoid interactions, he slipped into the foyer after the doors had already been closed by the ushers. The prospect of speaking to congregation members that knew him made him want to retreat, but he knew he was being irrational. He wanted to avoid feeling judgmental stares or pressure to return. He wasn't even sure what his quarrels were anymore, only that he wanted to avoid confronting them.

Entering the foyer, he was greeted by a doorman who he recognized distantly from years before. The man handed him the order of mass. Clapping his shoulder, he said quietly. "Good to have you back, old chap." Placide simply nodded his thanks and continued to the sanctuary doors.

Once he entered the sanctuary, he found a seat in the rear most pew and took it. As he shuffled into the seat, a young woman in the row before him turned to glance at him over her shoulder. She had a small baby in her arms that eyed him with wonder as she whispered. "Happy Christmas, Monsieur Cappeau. It's good to see you again." Her sincerity evident in the way she smiled without expectation. He returned the sentiment.

Placide opened the program for the first time, scanning to see where they were in the worship. Based on the snippet he heard of the prior song, he supposed they were nearing the scripture readings. The congregation began readings of the prophet Isaiah, followed by praise in David's Psalms, which ended in brief lines foreshadowing judgment and the need for cleansing. He imagined Père Gilles picked that tone to accompany the song, which was a nice touch.

A passage from Titus followed, bringing Christ's triumph over wickedness into sharper focus. Placide was wringing his hands as he tried to overcome his feelings of conviction. As each passage outlined the very thing he believed, he was forced to confront his own idea of the Church. This image, of his own construction, contrasted starkly with what he knew to be true.

The liturgy shifted to the birth story, the passage from Luke an obvious choice. Père Gilles read of the virgin birth and the humble setting. He emphasized the praises coming from the holy hosts. At the designated moment, the congregation spoke in unison, "Praise to you, Lord Jesus Christ." Placide found himself speaking the words too.

The congregation continued, moving to the words of a creed ingrained into Placide so deeply that he found comfort in speaking them with those around him. From there they proclaimed the belief in Father and Son, light from light, and in the Spirit. His eyes were closed as he continued. Words of death, burial, and the resurrection. Then, of course, the ascension to the right hand of God.

But when they arrived at the lines about the Spirit's inter-cession with prophets, his eyes sprang open, scanning the faces around him, finding Père Gilles' eyes at the front of the sanctuary. The most imperceptible glimmer in Père Gilles' eyes told Placide that he had seen him and was watching him. Père Gilles' mouth had the upward turn at the edges of the smile he tried to conceal, but it wavered as they approached the line that Placide would not speak: "I believe in one, holy, Catholic and Apostolic church."

Placide felt an unpleasant sense of disappointment wash over him as he recognized this would hurt Père Gilles, which hurt him too. Why did he still want to make Père Gilles proud? He searched for something, anything around him in which to ground himself as his mind began to spiral by its inability to understand his feelings towards these people, this place. He fumbled with the program, praying to find some kind of solace in the order. Instead he found that the offering was to be passed next. A chill struck him as clarity found him once more, granted to him by the demon of frustration and pettiness. Confronting him in that moment was also the prospect of partaking in the Lord's table directly afterwards. He was afraid that in the best case, people would silently judge his participation. But in the worst case, they would deny serving him altogether.

Though Placide found comfort in the welcome he received, something continued to gnaw at him with each passing moment seated in the sanctuary. Just because they were cordial, what guaranteed that would continue? Especially when the sacraments were introduced. Or when the song was performed. Surely their true nature would show once they'd heard who penned the song. They would think he'd repented, seen the error of his ways. But his thoughts had not shifted. He still heard the echo of his father's voice from childhood, emphasizing the lack of their own ownership, and the responsibility to steward their things well.

A growing buzz began in his feet, manifesting in his hands and arms, before finally zooming to his head. When Père Gilles asked everyone to bow in prayer for the offering, Placide seized the chance to rise from his seat and sulked into the foyer. He stepped into into an unoccupied hallway nearby and leaned his back into the wall. He inhaled quickly three or four breaths before sliding down the wall and into a seated position on the floor.

He pressed his ear towards the wall, hearing the blessing of the sacraments being administered. The blessing of the broken body, the spilled blood. How Placide had missed the imagery. His eyes welled with tears as he heard the shuffling of feet as the elements were served. Of the rituals and expectations that he had debated so vigorously with Père Gilles, the Lord's table was never one of them. It was the one that felt the most humbling, the most inviting to the throne of God for a lowly sinner like him. He whispered the *Amen* and crossed himself, clenching his eyes as he attempted to stifle the tears.

When Placide opened his eyes, a man he did not recognize was kneeling before him, holding a plate with the body and a cup with the blood. Placide's eyes must have shown his confusion as the man gestured the elements towards Placide. With trembling hands, Placide took first the bread, pausing for prayer, then the wine. Once he had finished, he gave the man a look of gratitude.

The stranger placed the tray and cup on the ground beside him, remaining crouched before Placide. He gently placed a hand on Placide's shoulder and bowed his head. His eyes were closed for nearly a minute, his lips soundlessly moving as if speaking. While he did so, Placide stared at him in wonder, a portion of his heartache escaping for an instant. Then, with a final squeeze of the shoulder, the stranger stood and left Placide.

He did not take the tray nor cup with him, disappearing as suddenly as he'd arrived.

Following the quiet, wordless movements of the conclusion of serving, Placide heard the creak of the stage flooring as a dozen people gathered. He heard Adolphe's voice address the audience. "Neither I nor my co-writer would take credit for the work that is about to be performed. We are merely the ones to report on the good message and inspiration of the Spirit among us. Our prayer is that you allow it to pierce your hearts as it did ours."

Placide heard the collective breath of the ensemble, but nothing else. As the piece began, he was struck once more with the intense fear of what the congregation might think. Would they heed the message, or even allow it to finish? What if they found out he was the one who helped create it? And poor Adolphe, how could he exist in the congregation after such a slight to them. He couldn't stand the thought of witnessing the crowd's reaction, of receiving their viperous response. He pulled himself to his feet, inched towards the door to the street, and paused in the doorway. He turned his head towards the sanctuary doors, wondering if the path he had begun could include them. Then, he faced the snow-laden street to examine the midnight hue, a winter breeze stirring.

The attendees of the midnight mass would later rave of the beauty of Adolphe's arrangement, the unity of the choir, organ, and vocalist. They would recall the heavenly ringing that sounded as the chords ascended the rafters and rebounded back. Publications would even laud the song as a beautiful glimmer in which the heavens resound.

Afterwards, when approached with praises and questions, Adolphe would not reveal his co-writer, but each time he was asked of who aided him, he would simply encourage the questioner to offer a prayer for the soul who gave the words.

Boston 2005

Bryn's hands were clenched tightly to his chest as he rocked in a defensive ball on the floor of his office. A bystander could easily assume a cardiac event if they were to hear his symptoms; chest tightening, arms tingling, shortness of breath. But Bryn knew better. He was no stranger to the predatory blindsides of his own panic. The not-so-self sabotage had affected him many times, always when it could cause the most damage. That's why when he felt it come on, the loss of fine motor function and breathlessness, he swiftly darted from the holding area backstage to his office. At least he had privacy on the carpet of his office floor as he waited for the feelings to pass.

What had he been thinking? Why had he changed so many things in the past week? He did not wonder that he had become consumed by the dread, only surprised that it had waited until this moment. He had completely changed the arrangement and rid the orchestra of Hall's presence. Then, 48 hours before the show, Charles asked him to sing the lead vocals for *O Holy Night*, conspiring with the Associate Conductor to helm the piece. It was too much, too soon and something had to give. His sanity appeared to be an unfortunate tribute.

Funnily enough, the anxiety hadn't manifested until he saw people picking up tickets at the box office a few hours earlier, putting faces to the abstract audience that had rarely entered his thoughts. It began when he noticed his fingers struggling to hold the baton steady. His fingers would not cooperate as he attempted to tie his bow tie either, soon abandoning the effort, unbuttoning his top button for relief.

His vision was obstructed by the moisture. This one felt more severe than others. He clinched his eyes shut in an effort to stop the tears, but each time he felt small drops of moisture fall on his cheek, he knew the flow would not stop just because he wanted them to. So he sat, alone on his office floor, the only light pouring in from the unshaded window that overlooked the city. Slowly, he felt the pounding in his chest soften.

He wiped his sleeve across his face, smearing tears, sweat, and nasal drip. He scanned the room, squinting to see the clock on the opposite wall. Thank goodness it was large, for he was able to just make out the time: a half hour to showtime. He knew that he had to pull himself together quickly, because he needed to tie his bow-tie and give his eyes the chance to lose some of their puff. But could he hold his baton? Could he face the audience?

The office door opened quietly. Charles entered. When he saw Bryn on the floor, he crossed to the piano bench and took a seat. He crossed his legs and faced Bryn, his gaze not lingering or passing judgment. More than anything, his glance was curious.

Bryn could see that it was up to him to break the silence. He allowed his body to relax a moment or two longer before clearing his throat, speaking weakly. "I don't think I can do this."

Charles said nothing, merely nodding in acknowledgment. Bryn spoke again, "It's just too much. I don't know why I let myself get talked into this."

Again, Charles nodded. He turned his body slightly away from Bryn to consider the keys on the piano. Slowly, gently, his right hand played the melody to the Scottish tune, *Loch Lomond*. Eventually, he spoke as he continued to play. "Remember when the guys learned this? Dr. Lowery had us learn it during sophomore year, right?"

"Yeah, everyone but you loved it. I still don't get what your problem was with that song."

Charles gave a small laugh. "I liked it at first, but then there was that rehearsal he sat us down and went through the meaning of the whole thing. He talked about the two Scottish soldiers imprisoned. One was going to be set free and the other executed. The one to be executed was comforting his comrade, telling him no matter what, in life or spirit, they would return to the homeland together again."

Bryn chuckled, forgetting himself for a moment. "That's beautiful, what's your problem?"

Charles feigned defensiveness in his amused response. "I thought that was such a cop out. I thought what if that were you and me. I'll tell you one thing, I wouldn't leave you to die if you gave me some line like that. You'd be coming with me, and I hope you'd do the same. I thought neither of us would give up and leave the other behind. But then I got older and realized that's the same sentiment the soldier is saying in the song, just steeped in reality instead of the cavalier ignorance I was living in." Charles laughed at himself.

Bryn laughed too. "So you hated it for years, even though you agreed with the sentiment, only less poetically?"

"Pretty much," Charles said with mild embarrassment. He dropped his gaze. "I was so frustrated by it, I didn't even sing at the concert. I was just moving my lips." At that admission, both men burst into loud, boisterous laughter. They continued for a minute before they faded off. Bryn noticed his heart had returned to a normal resting rate.

Charles faced Bryn, less amused. "The point I want to make is that I'm here for you, through it all. Also, I believe in you dearly, and this arrangement is your best work yet. Everything that is panicking you right now, all of it, is perfect. Now go show this audience what wonderful art I know you've made."

Bryn stood up, brushing his shirt. "Thank you, my well-intentioned if less poetic friend."

Both men walked towards the door, Charles giving Bryn a pat on the back. "I'm excited for people to be reminded how wonderful this song is."

Bryn smiled. "Maybe it can remind people how wonderful the reason for Christmas is too." As he reached for the knob to close his office door, he paused, hand suspended before him. He was pleased to see that it remained steady, unwavering in his control, confirming to himself that he was ready.

...

The residual ringing in Bryn's ear was eventually drowned out by the applause of the crowd. Taking a bow and shaking the first chair's hand, he mounted the platform and opened his score. He raised his arms, both baton and hand holding steadily, his eyes quickly scanning the musicians. He found them attentive and hungry for the concert to begin, no signs of fear in their pupils. When he was satisfied, having made sure everyone was ready, he signaled the first measure of the show.

And then they were off. Each member played masterfully,

Bryn noted. He heard the skill they were known for and the heart they had become masters of. The crowd cheered loudly at the end of each and every piece, continually anticipating each cascading note, welcoming every breath. Though the musicians maintained their expected professional poise, their eyes beamed with excitement. Their excitement was eventually returned to them by the audience. Then came the moment: *O Holy Night*.

Bryn stepped down from the platform, passing the baton to the Associate conductor who offered a warm, reassuring smile. He walked toward stage right to position himself in front of the microphone designated for his feature. Nerves made his hands slip into his pockets without thought, but when he realized, he quickly removed them. He felt the vulnerability, the openness between himself and the audience, no music stand, no baton. It had been nearly a decade since he had faced an audience to perform, his back normally what they saw most. Despite the pit growing in his stomach, he nodded to the conductor.

He found comfort, once he thought about it. The comfort rooted in hearing his friends play along with him, the arrangement bearing his evident fingerprints. Comfort in looking at the audience before him and immediately seeing Charles' beaming expression shining back. Comfort in the power of the piece they each had a hand in bringing to life, a piece whose lyrics proclaimed faithfulness in the coming Christ. The lyrics reminded him how deeply he hoped he, and others, would pursue the faithfulness described.

As the cellos began, Bryn found a quiet prayer slipping from his lips. "Spirit, make me your vessel so that these people may hear words honoring you." On his cue, he began the verse. He began the familiar words of a Savior's birth and a soul's worth echoing clearly. It was during the second verse that he noticed a peace that had entered him fully. As he began the lines of allowing faith and a star to lead, wise men searching for a king in a small manger, he felt a gentle hand leading him. He thought of the deliverance through such faith, beginning to sing a touch louder.

He had not thought about his eyes closing, but they had at some point during the second verse. By the third, he pried them open to see the audience. His eyes found more than just Charles staring back at him, but many other beautiful moments. He saw members with their own eyes closed, their mouths speaking the same words he was. Some held their hands to their chest, while others elevated them slightly. He saw parents holding their children, who also knew the words. Hands held in embrace as some members smiled, while others still allowed their tears to fall unashamed.

The key change approached, the majestic chorus ringing a final time. As the melody ascended to the climax of the line, each voice rose without strain in one accord. As a collective, they lingered on that singularly brilliant note, holding even after the instruments had dropped out. It was this unity observed in everyone that caused them to hold their applause for a moment when the song had finished, not wanting their unified breath to escape too suddenly.

Only when the moment was broken did they each breathe in their own time, clapping and applauding wildly. They clapped not for the orchestra or the vocals, but in celebration of the shared art they had each made, their hearts together in one worship.

Coda

Brant Rock 1906

Reginald Fessenden thumbed through the pages of his worn and tattered bible, searching for the passage that had immediately filled his thoughts. He stopped when he had reached the Gospel of Luke, turning to the second chapter.

"I pray everyone who has heard this broadcast has a blessed Christmas. If you care to let us know where you heard us from, send us a letter. This is still new technology, so any message helps. It's easy to forget why we celebrate this season, so if you don't mind, I would like to read from the second chapter of Luke.

" 'For unto you is born this day in the city of David a Savior, which is Christ the Lord. And this shall be a sign to you; ye shall find the babe wrapped in swaddling clothes, lying in a manger. And suddenly there was with the angel a multitude of the heavenly host praising God and saying, 'Glory to God in the highest, and on earth peace, good will toward men.' "

Fessenden closed his bible, speaking into the microphone a final time. "Merry Christmas, everyone. May the peace of the Lord and his goodness abound in you forever and ever."

Appendix I: The Historical Connections of O Holy Night

Roquemaure 1847 - In December of 1847, wine merchant Placide Cappeau met with his local priest on his way to Paris for business. The sanctuary had recently undergone renovations, including improvements to its organ. A known poet in his spare time, the priest requested Placide write something for the Christmas service. Placide wrote the majority of a poem, titled "Minuit, chrétiens" (Midnight, Christians), on his six-hour carriage ride to Paris.

The poem was presented to Adolphe Adam, a successful composer, to arrange for performance. Adolphe's arrangement was performed at the Midnight Mass by a mutual friend to all three: Opera singer Madame Laurey. She performed the piece, accompanied by the newly renovated organ. The piece was received well by all attendees, but in later years, was scrutinized due to its authors.

Placide Cappeau apostatized later in life, his views no longer conforming to those recognized by the Roman Catholic Church. While unclear what specifically caused the shift in Cappeau, it is widely known that tensions formed between Catholic officials and Cappeau around the time of the Revolutions of 1848. Considering his Jesuit upbringing, along with how the tone of the piece appeared in conjunction with the Revolution, proved enough concern for the Catholic Church to distance themselves from the song.

Adolphe Adam, although unknown if he was raised with any religious affiliation, often performed in churches across France. Many rumors were started to discredit the authors or their legitimacy as grounds for removing the song. Because of his profession in wine trading, Cappeau was labeled a drunkard. Adolphe Adam was incorrectly labeled as Jewish, which unfortunately in that setting subjected him to prejudice as well. Despite the friction, Adolphe Adam converted to Catholicism at some point in his later years and was given a Roman Catholic funeral service upon his passing.

Boston 1855 - John Sullivan Dwight earned his degree in Ministry from the Harvard School of Divinity, but his career as a minister was short-lived. He quickly discovered a love for music, taking a job as a teacher where he taught music and theater. During this time, he began writing a periodic music column containing reviews and general content regarding music.

Dwight continued to enjoy writing reviews for local publications about shows and pieces he had witnessed. As his readership steadily grew, he eventually went on to found "Dwight's Journal of Music" in 1852. The publication became one of the most popular periodicals in the country at the time, marking him as one of the first music critics in the country.

In 1855, while researching pieces to include in the winter edition of his publication, Dwight discovered *O Holy Night*, written in the original French. He translated the piece for his publication, while taking some liberties with certain phrases, especially those regarding slavery. A known abolitionist, his liberal alterations to the lines pertaining to slaves and brotherhood made the song the anthem it is known as today.

Brant Rock 1906 - Reginald Fessenden was a Canadian-American engineer responsible for hundreds of patents in the electronic communications space, specifically in radio transmission and reception. One major contribution to the industry came with his company's implementation of an alternator-transmitter, which gave rise to the eventual ability for radio to be more wide-reaching than before. AM radio, entertainment radio, and telecommunications are all modern staples that can be traced to the works of Fessenden.

Though documentation of the Brant Rock radio test in December 1906 depicts the achievements of the trial, the time and actual contents of the message conveyed is less certain. There is still no confirmation as to if the true test came on December 21 or December 24. Additionally, some speculate that *O Holy Night* was the first commercially broadcast song, but no definitive proof has survived in the century since the broadcasts. The claim was perpetuated by Fessenden's confirmation of such during many written correspondences in the following years and has been widely accepted.

Appendix II: Complete Lyrics of 'O Holy Night'

O holy night, the stars are brightly shining;
it is the night of the dear Savior's birth.
Long lay the world in sin and error pining,
till He appeared and the soul felt its worth.
A thrill of hope, the weary world rejoices,
for yonder breaks a new and glorious morn!
Fall on your knees! O hear the angel voices!
O night divine! O night when Christ was born!
O night divine! O night, O night divine!

Led by the light of faith serenely beaming,
with glowing hearts by His cradle we stand.
So led by light of a star sweetly gleaming,
there came the wise men from Orient land.
The King of kings lay thus in lowly manger;
in all our trials born to be our friend.
He knows our need, to our weakness is no stranger.
Behold your King; before Him lowly bend!
Behold your King; before Him lowly bend!

Truly He taught us to love one another;
His law is love and His gospel is peace.

Chains shall He break, for the slave is our brother,
and in His name all oppression shall cease.
Sweet hymns of joy in grateful chorus raise we,
let all within us praise His holy name.
Christ is the Lord! O praise His name forever!
His pow'r and glory evermore proclaim!
His pow'r and glory evermore proclaim!

Afterward

I began this project in the most embarrassing way: as a distraction. For 15 months, I worked tirelessly on the first draft of a novel that took a lot out of me. I finished my first draft in September of 2024, took a two-week break, then began first round edits on it. But by late October, having edited the first 80 pages, I felt the need to step back from the material. I still wanted to write, but knew that I wanted to spend a few months on something different. I started sifting through some drafts of old projects and found research notes that I had intended for an essay about *O Holy Night*. With Christmas around the corner, that felt like a nice change of pace.

I continued to look through my notebooks to see what other half-baked ideas I had written down. I'd had the skeleton of a scene with a conductor (Bryn) having a panic attack before a concert. I had notes about a newspaper editor (John Sullivan) working through the night because he was so in love with a play. I'd had dialogues of two people (Adolphe and Placide) discussing the drop in church attendance simply because of the people's judgment. Thankfully, each idea came organically.

I knew I wanted to focus on the stories of Placide Cappeau, Adolphe Adam, John Sullivan Dwight, and Reginald Fessenden, but I didn't know how to tell them considering the four didn't have any interaction with one another. I knew a nontraditional structure would be necessary to juggle the timelines, so I explored different options. I wrote the piece chronologically, beginning with Roquemaure, then to Boston, Brant Rock, and Boston again. It was in writing the 2005 Boston story that the idea for symphonic movements came about.

Though traditionally performed with only an instrument or two, the four movement sonata form of symphony music followed the tempo and thematic trajectory that I wanted this story to experience. Identifying the movements helped in finding the right pacing. As I began to cut the stories to fit within the four movements, I found that each movement needed a short breath before concluding, which is where the short vignettes came from. Movements I-III end with a one-off story to cleanse the palate before the following movement begins. Movement IV begins with one of these vignettes in order to retell the birth story, which seemed vital to include in the finale.

I worked obsessively for someone trying to distract themselves. I wrote after work and while I ate lunch most days. I would listen to symphony music while I ran and in the car, plotting the story in my head. Shout out to Boston Pops Orchestra; they were a huge inspiration. I would be thinking of the characters as I went to bed, occasionally dreaming of the scenes that eventually made their way onto the page. I loved every second of working on this. In a way, this project has spoiled me because it came unnaturally fast, in a way I doubt will happen again. But it was the experience I needed following the 15 month novel. This book reminded me why I love writing so much.

This story holds so many moments and details that are special to me. Themes of music, creating art, crisis of faith, and deep male friendships are all themes close to my heart and I'm thankful to have had an arena to explore them. Bryn's panic attack before a show, Adolphe's frank conversations with Placide, and the inclusion of Loch Lomond bear a significance to me that I will forever be proud to have put in print. And I consider the Tennessee vignette to be my favorite thing I've written so far.

O Holy Night is such a special song. It's the perfect vessel for everyone to appraise where they are in their own faith walk and see where to continue. It shows the holiness and humanity of Christ as well as how necessary and life-saving his presence is. I found studying this song to be deeply inspiring, and I hope others can find themselves with a refreshed view as well.

Little Rock - June 2025

Acknowledgments

The best art comes through influence, collaboration, and discovery with those around you. Hopefully, such was evident in the stories presented. The friendships between Bryn and Charles or Adolphe and Placide illustrate that every artist is made better when those around them engage with the process, encourage, and challenge us to grow further. Artists are sensitive beings, but flourish when others resonate in their expression.

Special thanks to the communities around me whose interests and kind words offered continued encouragement when the process of this project seemed daunting. Namely, our congregation at Windsong Church of Christ, my work community at EAST, and the connections from my alma maters. For such a solitary act as writing, I never once felt I was on this journey alone.

Thank you to Matt Dozier for pouring over these pages with a fresh set of eyes and making impactful and insightful suggestions and critiques. Much like Adolphe's interpolation of Placide's words, Matt helped find a story that spoke more plainly to what I wanted to say but could have never found on my own. This book is infinitely better because his fingerprints are on it too.

Thank you to Kelley Klein and Rochelle Klein for their feedback as first readers. By the time they'd set eyes on it, I'd become completely unable to see this work with a fresh set of eyes. Their feedback and suggestions were both encouraging and eye opening. They helped me make the subtle changes I otherwise was blind to but can now see were infinitely important.

Thank you to Gracie Perry for a spectacular cover design. When faced with the challenge of creating a cover for this work, she graciously accepted and created what I feel to be the perfect representation for this book. I'd never collaborated with a cover artist before and she made the entire process a wonderful experience, making me feel both heard and understood. This is one of the times I hope people do judge a book by it's cover: they will really think this book is spectacular if they do!

Thank you to Matt Johnson, Josh Girndt, Jesse Russell, and Jonathan Lancaster, to whom this book is dedicated. I was fourteen when Josh and I stumbled into choir as freshman. It was there that Mr. Johnson showed us why music is special, why art is vital, and why creativity is the greatest key to understanding what makes us tick. A few years after our introduction to choir, Josh, Jesse, Jonathan, and I sang in a quartet and loved every second of making music together. It's these experiences and relationships that I pray is represented with respect and reverence in the characters I wrote. The only thing more beautiful than making music is making music with your friends.

I am grateful for the lives of Placide Cappeau, Adolphe Adam, John Sullivan Dwight, and Reginald Fessenden. Without any one of them, this historic song would not exist. Time is the greatest judge of impact, and I'm certain the impact of *O Holy Night* is evident by the regard it still holds over 150 years later.

Mountains and mountains of thanks to my wife Ansley. She has always been my first audience, my biggest supporter, and the push I need to chase down the made up stories that the characters in my head get themselves into. Any discipline I have as a writer is only because she sees my passion and encourages me to put in the work. I like to say that I write the stories I would love to read, but that's only partly true. The stories are just as much hers as they are mine.

And of course, the greatest thank you of all is for the thrill of hope we each are given. God, in His infinite love for us, made us in His image. Yet even after we tainted our relationship with Him with our selfishness, He gave us a hope for redemption through Jesus. It is that hope that restores our perfect relationship with our Creator forever.

About the Author

Dawson Cumberland is a non-profit accountant in Little Rock, Arkansas. He has a passion for reading books much too large and writing stories for much too long. He lives there with his wife and their pup, Tuck. Previous works include the novella *Meet Me When the Road Ends*.